SOME RUN CROOKED

John Buxton Hilton

St Martin's Press
New York

Copyright ©1978 by John Buxton Hilton

All rights reserved. For information, write:
St. Martin's Press, Inc., 175 Fifth Ave., New York,
N.Y. 10010

Printed in Great Britain

Library of Congress Catalog Card Number: 77–10182

First published in the United States of America in 1978

Library of Congress Cataloging in Publication Data

Hilton, John Buxton
    Some run crooked.

    I. Title
PZ4.H6568So   1978   [PR6058.I5]   823'.9'14
ISBN 0–312–74355–6   77–10182

HISTORICAL NOTE

Some readers may like help in distinguishing the fact from the fiction in this story. The marriage facilities in the *Peculiar Court of Peak Forest* remain today as outlined by a spokesman of the County Constabulary in the opening chapter. The fuller facts are well documented by various writers, amongst them Crichton Porteous in *Portrait of the Peak* (Robert Hale). Peak Forest is a reality; the village of Peak Low, with its chapel of ease, is an invention, as are its inhabitants and the violence done there.

In 1758 an eloping couple were nastily murdered in the Winnats Pass on their way to Peak Forest; vide Brian Spencer: *Castleton, Edale and Kinder Scout* (Moorland Publishing Company). I have taken this as a suggestion rather than a model. It may well not have been an isolated instance.

J.B.H.

CHAPTER ONE

As a rule, Kenworthy said, murder was too drearily reasonable for words. But he wasn't levelling that criticism at this one for long. A killing two hundred years ago; its carbon copy within the clear memory of our own generation; and now this one. And a strange woman, who became stranger the more we learned about her; a marriage facility that we had to explain afresh every time we mentioned it.

It was in the late 1950s that we went up into the remoteness of north-west Derbyshire, Kenworthy and I. They were vintage years that we were living through, though we did not always realise it at the time. The Beatles had not yet emerged. The nadir of the un-respectable was an energetic work-out known as Rock 'n' Roll. In police fiction the image was still Dixon. *Z Cars* were not yet on the studio floor. Personal radios for beat bobbies were still a localised experiment. Task forces and serious-crime squads weren't commonly talked about. But at least in the eyes of the public at large a tale of a bent copper was still barely credible.

In this world it was still not unusual for a Yard inspector and his sergeant to be sent on safari. Chief Constables called on help from various motives: subor-dinates' rivalries and Watch Committee politics were not always very skilfully concealed. But in the case of Julie Wimpole there was a certain straightforwardness about the preambles that threw the onus fairly and unarguably on Kenworthy's shoulders and mine.

Nobody knew who Julie Wimpole was. She had had problems: but they lay far away from the inward-looking communities of Peak Low, Peak Forest and Peak Dale. Well, so it seemed . . .

I say, on Kenworthy's shoulders and mine, but if anything went wrong, no one was going to throw the book at anyone but Kenworthy. I was a very new sergeant, and this was my first excursion into frontier territory with him: an alarming prospect, yet I was as excited as a schoolboy who sees his name as a reserve for the first eleven. Excited – but careful: there was a club of sergeants who had only been out with Kenworthy once.

From St Pancras to Leicester he remained immersed in his newspaper; from Leicester to Derby he talked. And never have I paid greater attention to steering clear of slack answers. Kenworthy was still a comparatively young inspector – though was the man ever *young* within the meaning of the act? He already had scalps under his belt – from both sides of the law. Intolerance was a plank in his platform. In all his opinions he shunned consistency. On politics and league football, on race-horses, celebrities and religion he was unpredictable – but never less than forceful. He created about himself a wilful state of confusion in which men sometimes carelessly let slip morsels of truth about themselves.

'They call you Shiner.'

So they had, during my National Service. But it was Kenworthy who resurrected the idiotic label and made it stick. There were times when his sense of humour could be puerile; notably when he was bored, more especially when he was jittery about something that might jump either way. But it had not occurred to me, in those days, that Kenworthy could ever jitter.

8

'There's only one way to shine on a job like this, Sergeant Wright.'

'Sir?'

'We shall need the luck of the nine blind bastards,' Kenworthy said.

I have never known the history of those egregious gentlemen, nor have I grasped the point at which fortune is supposed to have favoured them. But Kenworthy invoked them from time to time, usually as an alternative to saying anything more committal. The safest riposte was tacit agreement, pretending that one still found the image amusing. In any case, one had a rough idea what he meant.

From Derby onwards we were carried in a county car: northwards, alongside a river that tumbled between slopes of yellowing ash plantations. It was early November, a clammy, silent, lifeless day down in the valley bottoms, with dead leaves clinging dispiritedly to wet roads.

'People come here to get married, you know. Well, hardly ever nowadays, but they can if they want to.'

The voice of our county pilot droned flatly on.

'The Chief Super has asked me to put you in the picture. I'm afraid it means a spot or two of ancient history.'

Kenworthy listened without comment.

'In 1657, it was: a long time to go back. And it was a bad time for brave gestures. But the then Dowager Countess of Devonshire had a mind of her own. She was an ardent royalist. Her son had been killed in the king's service. So she founded a chapel at Peak Forest, in the name of Saint Charles, King and Martyr. It was outside the jurisdiction of the bishops, and the priest was called *Principal Official and Judge in Spiritualities in the Peculiar Court of Peak Forest*. He had a lot of power,

9

including the right to solemnise marriage according to a liberal set of rules. And when a chapel of ease was built at Peak Low in the 1730s, his writ extended there as well. In the first part of the eighteenth century the place was very popular amongst runaway couples – and a source of welcome income for the vicar. No questions were asked of bride and bridegroom other than their names. The sole requirement was that one of them should have resided in the parish for fifteen days.'

He paused for our questions. We had none.

'There was an average of some sixty marriages a year until 1753, when a new Marriage Act made some attempt to get them under control; not with total success, however, for there were entries in the Register as late as 1804. Then at last they seemed to think the practice was defeated.'

1804. We were getting warmer.

'It wasn't the end, though. In 1938 a new vicar announced that he thought it healthier for an eloping couple to marry before an altar rather than over an anvil. He made it known that he was going to revive the old facilities. Two marriages followed, and then he was taken in front of a diocesan court as a test case.'

'We're into the 1940s, then?'

'It came as a surprise to a lot of people in the early years of the war when the tribunal came down in favour of this little pocket of independence. Nothing, the judges said, could be done to prevent the Vicar of Peak Forest from marrying *whomsoever they be and whence-soever they come at any reasonable time*. And so it still is, though little known about and even less used.'

We had by now climbed to heights where the trees were fewer and already bare: dry-stone walls enclosing narrow, barren, irregular rectangles of rock-strewn fields. Peak Low was mostly a single cross-roads, a cluster of grey squat cottages which had happened into the landscape as fungus springs from a damp old log. Along the roads visibility was not too bad, perhaps a hundred and fifty yards. Across country the mist was more apparent. The nearest spinney, a skeletal outpost of sycamore and elm, was cloaked almost to the point of extinction. Beyond it, other clumps of trees and a line of great hills were something that one sensed rather than saw.

Kenworthy had the car stop on a corner of descending lane which gave us our first commanding view of the settlement. Time spent in reconnaissance, he was never tired of reminding us, was seldom wasted. But in this case reconnaissance was no more ambitious than a three-yard walk along the grass verge to lean our elbows on the top bar of a rotting gate. There was something in the atmosphere that seemed to immobilise even the smoke from domestic hearths; it hung close to damp slate roofs as if it were reluctant to disperse.

'Fifteen nights in this bloody hole,' Kenworthy said. 'That must have given second thoughts to many a Romeo.'

CHAPTER TWO

Julie Wimpole was judged to be a little over the thirty mark – by the village on her arrival and the pathologist on her departure. For a fortnight she had lived in Peak Low under the public eye – an eye admiring, scathing, scornful, even here and there open-minded – but un-remitting; and even the more sympathetic observers would have needed little persuasion to become destructive. A red, labouring service bus had brought her juddering over the parish boundary and in general Peak Low was inclined to be critical of an unescorted nubile female who appeared content to organise her own solitude.

Nubile: Julie Wimpole was undoubtedly attractive, in an unexceptional, unaggressive, unexotic way. Those in Peak Low who still had eyes for nubile females did not see many samples within their own boundaries, except at weekends for creatures in bobbed caps, anoraks and fell-boots, who were often indistinguishable from their men-folk against the flanks of the hills. Julie was brunette, hair frequently (and recently) washed, height five feet four, small hands tightly gloved, spectacles in translucent frames that might have crabbed her appearance but didn't, dressed mostly but newly by Marks and Spencer. She looked back with unoffended interest at the men who frankly examined her. She was perfectly ordinary, and yet she drew attention wherever she appeared. There was nearly a fight about her before she was fairly off the bus. There was something not quite strange yet frustratingly indefinable about her: all the witnesses, varyingly articulate, were agreed about that.

'She looked,' someone said, 'strangely sure of herself, yet you could see underneath that she wasn't.'

'There was something different about her, something that set her apart, yet you couldn't put your finger on it. Not that I'm saying there was any side to her. Far from it. She was only too ready to be friends with everybody – in the public bar or in the lounge. You got the feeling that if you put her down in the right company, she could be a bit of a lass.'

That was Bill Hepplewhite, landlord of the *Three Horseshoes*.

'She took an interest in everything she set eyes on. Well, it was something more than an interest. She was *alive* – God, what am I saying? – but I mean it. She *was* alive. There was something in her eyes, a sort of light. She was on fire about things, everyday things, about every little thing that came her way.'

'Like as if everything interested her – quarrying, and stone-crushing, and the furnaces, and the history of the place, and the old Powder Mill, and politics, and juvenile delinquents, and skiffle, and Drydale.'

'Especially Drydale.'

It was in Drydale that she had gone to her death. And so had two others, one twenty, one two hundred years before her.

'Well, you'd expect her to take an interest in the place, wouldn't you, being here for the reason she was?'

'But we didn't know for certain why she was here, Mr Kenworthy, though of course there was wedding talk. Some of us thought she was just here on holiday, though it was a funny time of year for it.'

'She didn't go out much, for someone on holiday.'

'Well, yes, she did, you know, Jack. She went out quite a bit. She went down Drydale for a start – more than once. But not always at the time of day you'd have expected. And she did seem to stay indoors a lot – even when the weather ought to have tempted her out.'

'You'd almost have thought she knew something was going to happen.'

'She knew a good deal more than she cared to let on. That's obvious, when you come to look back.'

'She knew about Drydale.'

'And about the Powder Mill.'

'And about why people come to Peak Low.'

'You mean why they used to.'

'You still can, you know, Jack.'

'Yes, but who needs that sort of thing these days, with a Register Office round everyone's corner?'

'Never mind about who needs it. Some of them want it that way. Adds a bit of spice to life, you might say. Some of us reckoned, Mr Kenworthy, that she was here waiting for a man. Only he never came. Or if he did, he'd a change of mind about her.'

'A bloody big change of mind.'

'Anyway, I don't think she was the stranger to Peak Low that she cracked on to be.'

This was the sort of conversational miasma that was eddying about us before Kenworthy and I had been in Peak Low much longer than an hour. Kenworthy had warned me not to be too ready with questions. Asking too many supplementaries in the initial stages, he said, put blinkers on people. If they thought we were getting interested in some particular aspect, then they'd pull things to please us; and then we might miss something.

Some of the opinions we heard were more fanciful than others.

'I don't know how to put it. I did see a woman like her once, but it was in hospital, and she'd just been told there was no cure for her. Yet she was utterly resigned to it, utterly serene.'

Not that there had been anything sickly in Julie Wimpole's appearance; on the contrary, she was red-blooded with health. Her movements were brisk, her gestures crisp, her step nimble.

'It's difficult to describe. She was like a guest at a party who's been asked to get up and recite. And she doesn't want to. She's drifted away into a corner. She's struggling in her mind to remember the piece. Yet when the moment comes, she'll rise to it. Then afterwards she'll just be one of the crowd again.'

That was Constance Winstanley, Secretary of the Women's Institute, who read Rilke in translation and wrote poetry of her own, and had once had a sonnet published in a review.

Back in the pub they were concrete about their failure to place her.

'You'll not find a soul in the village, Mr Kenworthy, who has a notion as to what walk of life she came from. She took a positive delight in puzzling us. When we dropped hints, trying to get it out of her in a round-about way, she made it clear that she'd dug in her heels and wasn't going to tell us. All very friendly, you understand, as if it were some sort of game she were playing. And you could tell that she was a woman accustomed to having her own way. She was a damned sight too clever to let anything out by accident. In fact, sir, some of us thought at one stage that she might be in the same line of business as yourself. She seemed to know a lot about what goes on in the mind of a wrong 'un.'

'It seemed quite a hobby with her – Teds, and dropouts and wrong 'uns.'

One ineradicable peculiarity of Julie Wimpole had been the impediment in her speech. It was not so much a stammer, though she did sometimes have trouble over her initial consonants, as a constriction of the larynx that afflicted her when she was about to address a stranger for the first time, or to broach a new line of thought. She would have several shots at it, would jerk her head, furrow her brow, bite her lower lip. Then suddenly the word she wanted would tumble out, as if it had got itself out of a trap.

'It was a shame, because it spoiled her personality.

At least, it ought to have done, but it didn't really, if you see what I mean. In a way you were spellbound. You wanted to help her out, yet you couldn't. You mustn't. I'm not saying that it was something that she put on but, without being unkind, I'd say it was something she'd been cursed with, and yet learned to make the most of. You had to listen to her, because you had to wait for what was coming. And because you had to wait for it, you had to slow down your own thinking, and take the pace from her.

'But once she got going, it didn't seem to trouble her so much. She talked to us in here, the public bar at that, for an hour at a time, didn't she? It seemed there was no stopping her. Then as Bill says, she'd go off on some new tack and start spluttering again. It was worse when she was saying something she wasn't so sure about – or when she was trying to tread on our toes, coming out with something she meant us to disagree with. Some of her ideas took a lot of stomaching, you'll understand.'

'Especially in Peak Low.'

'Like her ideas about young people today.'

'The funny thing was, when she really got going, you'd have thought she must be somebody who actually talked for a living. A teacher, or something like that. Yet how could anyone with such a speech defect ever have got through to be a teacher?'

'She wasn't a teacher. She denied that most powerfully – seemed almost insulted when we suggested it.'

'In fact, she thought teachers had all got hold of the wrong end of the stick.'

'And young people today,' Kenworthy interposed gently. 'She was on their side, was she?'

'Oh, God, yes. They could do no wrong. Even those

in Borstal who were heading for real time. We thought for a while she must be a psychiatrist. Only she denied that, too. She was dead nuts against psychiatrists. Very much a law unto herself, was Miss Wimpole.'

A law unto herself, but she had been a thorn in some-one's flesh. She ended her days as a corpse from which kiln-hardened professionals averted their eyes. And Kenworthy was content to sit out our first evening in the public bar of the Shoes, grinning amiably, making a pint of mild and bitter last an hour and a half, agree-ing good-naturedly with contradictory opinions. We pressed no one, wrote nothing down, checked nothing against recorded statements.

'Hill folk, Shiner,' Kenworthy said, as we bumped shoulders in the unlit Peak Low night.

'Yes, sir.'

'No, sir. Don't let them fool you. Most of those men have had five years away from this midden. They've learned to be radio mechanics, asdic operators, sound-rangers and flash-spotters. They know enough words in six or seven languages to organise their crumpet in any latitude. They've carved Kilroy's name at the top of the Great Pyramid, they've liberated Tunis and Brussels. They listen to the B.B.C. and sometimes even read the inside pages of their newspapers.'

'Yes, sir.'

'And don't let that fool you, either. If ever they decided to stand together – if ever they thought there was something we ought not to find out, you and I, they'd remember a lot about how things used to be in the old days. How to keep your own counsel without being openly aggressive about it. They could set up a front, Shiner, and I wouldn't care to have it to bust.'

'No, sir.'
'Nine blind bastards, Shiner.'
'Quite, sir.'

CHAPTER THREE

She had arrived in Peak Low on the bus from Buxton,
wiping steam from the window with a tissue from her
bag, not with her finger-tips like most of the other
women, peering out into the formless fields in the
greying afternoon. At Fairfield and Upper End a
number of housewives got out and there was a general
post towards empty seats. But at the Quarries the
coach filled up again, a whiff of raw fog as the folding
doors opened, a blur of orange lights amongst concrete
girders, a rattle of stone as an automatic tipper up-
ended a hopper over a kiln, a mess of slithery lime-dust
gruel under the feet of slithering passengers. Most of
those who boarded here looked like clerical workers, a
gaggle of teen-aged girls with here and there a middle-
aged man in a threadbare office suit.

But the man who sat down at Julie Wimpole's side
was clearly part of the teeth and claws of the work
force: a cloth cap torn by rock-splinters, jacket and
trousers discarded from separate suits, a khaki pullover
from his army days, huge boots with leather laces
knotted about his ankles. He sat down beside her in an
aura of lime-dust, stale sweat and the acrid lingering
smoke of rock-face explosive.

'Finished for the week, now?'

She started talking to him the moment he lowered
himself to her side: a cheerful prattle that she did not

allow her stammer to inhibit: about his shift hours, and whether he ate his midday meal in a works canteen, about his hobbies (he did not appear to have any) and the leisure amenities of Peak Low (which were largely contained between the bar-counter and the dart-board).

Will Beard: it was coincidence and infelicity that made him the mentor of her arrival. He leaned his shoulder heavily into hers as he ferreted in his pocket for the scarred Elastoplast tin in which he kept his tobacco, rolled himself a saliva-stained cigarette and answered her questions monosyllabically, as if he thought that her curiosity was aimed somehow at his undoing.

Will Beard had a history; but when we came to try to get people to be precise about it, they proved less informed than they had suggested. It had been nearly twenty years ago, on the eve of the war, and had involved an adolescent girl in a sterile side-valley. There had been talk of indecent assault: Beard had been taken away to Chapel-en-le-Frith for the night, brought back again the next morning uncharged. It was variously said that the girl had withdrawn her allegations; that her father had made her do so; that she had made the whole thing up; that her story was true, but that they had suppressed it to save her from the witness-box. No one knew for certain, and no one had ever dared to press Will Beard for enlightenment. He had a long reach and a short temper. It was odd that Will should have been the one to take his seat next to Julie Wimpole: he was the one pillar of the Shoes whose leg no one dared pull about it.

Peak Low was the terminus and the bus cleared it-self, passengers' breath vaporous on the frosty air, feet scurrying away to havens of pale light behind rectangles of curtained window, hot water already warming brown earthenware tea-pots. Julie Wimpole stood on the kerb momentarily uncertain, her suit-case so heavy that she could barely get it off the ground. The doors of the bus clanked to behind her.

'Can you tell me the way to Starvelings – to Starvelings Farm?'

She had not attached herself particularly to Will Beard, nor, as far as we could prove, he to her, but he happened to be one of the last of the dispersing crowd. He reached down a rock-scarred hand and swung up her bag as if it had been empty.

'Show you the way. Carry this for you.'

He was not exactly a dullard, but reluctant of speech. We thought, on reconstruction, that he might have been touched by the interest she had shown in him. At any rate, he had become her devoted servant.

'That would be kind of you.'

But someone else, from whatever motive, also paid her attention.

'Evening, ma'am. Did I hear you say Starvelings? It's a devil of a walk up there, especially in shoes like yours. You're as likely as not to break your neck.'

He was a broad-shouldered man of about her own age, well dressed for the bus crowd, crisp curly hair well oiled, but slightly out of place in the evening air, a club scarf about his shoulders, on his lips an intimate smile that he had clearly never thought of as resistible.

'Evening, Mr Cantrell.'

Will Beard spoke, but still clung possessively to the case. Cantrell stretched out his hand towards it and Beard swung it defiantly away, looking to the woman for her decision.

'I'll tell you what,' Cantrell said. 'My wife's had the car all day. Hairdresser. That's why I was using the bus. But she'll be home by now. I can run you up round by the road in five minutes. I wouldn't take to the fields on an afternoon like this if I were you.'

Cantrell's story was that he intervened because he distrusted Beard, and that Julie Wimpole must surely find the quarryman repulsive. But he himself must have been more than usually interested in her, which says something for her impact. She cannot have appeared particularly exotic to Cantrell, who was evidently a man who fancied his chances. There was something about her that he found worthy of investigation. Cantrell's wife, we discovered, was in a more or less permanent anxiety state about their marriage.

'I'd prefer the footpath, thank you,' Julie Wimpole said. 'I've got a torch, and odd though it may seem, it's a walk I've been looking forward to for a long time.'

She looked down at her buckled brogues.

'And I'm better shod than you'd think. Sensible, I think, is the word.'

Will Beard was wary of talking about their walk across the fields, but Kenworthy was patient with him.

'She knew the way, yet she didn't know it. She'd an idea where Starvelings was, yet she'd never have found it on her own. She knew quite a bit about this place, but out of date. We passed Bracken Farm and she asked about the Keelings. Didn't know they'd sold out before the end of the war. Then she started asking questions about the Powder Mill.'

This was a mid-nineteenth-century ruin in a shallow declivity between fields – a straggle of stone sheds, now roofless, doorless and windowless. The site had been used for the manufacture of gunpowder since time unrecorded. It was rumoured that some of the broadsides that repelled the Armada had been mixed in this mill. Then, before contemporary memory, there had been an explosion that had reduced the complex to its present state. But at the lower end of the grounds, by an over-shot water-wheel, now crippled over a leaking weir, was the former overseer's house, which still appeared intact, though its windows were boarded over and rough cross-stanchions nailed across the front door.

'It interested her a lot,' Will Beard said.

'And what did you tell her about it?'

'What is there to tell? It stood empty before the war, then a school took it, which came from somewhere down south when the bombs were expected. Then they went away again, and the army had it. Now it stands empty, and to my mind it'll stay so. No one could afford the rates, let alone keep it warm. There are fire-places you could burn a five-barred gate in.'

Will Beard had led her past the Powder Mill and across the wooden, single-railed plank bridge at the head of Drydale, and so up a stony sheep-track to the yard of the farm known as Starvelings. He had carried her bag as far as the door, made a rudimentary gesture of touching his cap, and stepped back into the shadows, beyond the reach of the single electric light bulb shining over the step.

Whoever had christened the holding Starvelings had been cocking a snook at his own lunacy in trying to scrape a living from the exposed and thin-soiled hillside. We saw any number of such hill-farms: lean-ribbed store cattle, sheep that miraculously survived weeks of drifting snow, pumps that needed priming with hot water through abnormally long winters: holdings of parlous acreage, too small to be workable, too high above sea-level for a fruit tree or a field of grain.

Nevertheless, under the regime of David and Anne

Bagshaw, who had moved in from Cheshire with a war-time gratuity, the name Starvelings had become an irony. Kenworthy and I were struck – as Julie Wimpole must have been struck when the door was opened to her – by the affluence of the household. There were consumer goods of a quality exceptional for the decade. Already the Bagshaws were anticipating the time when people at large would have it as good as this: an automatic dish-washer, custom-built kitchen units, stainless steel predominating, a large-screen television set, aquaria of tropical fish, with all the latest gadgetry of filters, heaters and aerators.

It was not all the product of their farming. The Bagshaws had put capital into crumbling cottages up and down the village, renovated them and let them to summer visitors. The breakfasts that Anne Bagshaw provided for overnight visitors had become a legend; this year she had ventured into dinners as well. Always the helpings were monumental, the profit reasonable and secure. Moreover, David had worked single-handed throughout a winter to turn a suite of upstairs rooms into a self-contained flat – the one that Julie Wimpole had booked for a fortnight.

She had booked it by telephone, having seen it advertised in a northern provincial daily. She had paid the rent in advance by money order, stamped in a post office in central Manchester. Anne Bagshaw had been glad – and surprised – to let the room. The season was done, and she had a fortnight's gap before the arrival of a winter resident, a sabbatical historian who was hoping for lack of diversions from his writing.

Anne Bagshaw had liked Julie Wimpole so much at first sight that it came as a shock to her to realise, in the final count, how little she knew about her. The two women looked at each other as Julie was let into the

23

house, and at once there seems to have arisen a sympathetic bond between them, an unspoken agreement that questions were not going to be asked.

The suitcase was too heavy for either of them to carry up to the flat, and Anne Bagshaw asked how she had got it across the fields.

'A quarryman was kind enough to help me out.'

'Which quarryman?'

'I didn't ask his name. I heard someone call him Will. Though actually I was offered a lift round by the road.'

'I'd have opted for that, if I'd been in your shoes.'

'I was kicking myself, by the time we reached the Powder Mill. But I thought the man with the car was no more than a kerb-crawler.'

'You don't know who he was?'

'I heard him called Cantrell.'

Anne Bagshaw nodded, though she did not go so far as to slander a villager in front of a stranger. She took her tenant for a tour of cooker, knife drawer, shelves and gadgets. The rooms were cleanly decorated in cheap but cheerful wallpaper. Anne Bagshaw knew that she was giving good value for the rent, but was in some unease as Julie Wimpole stood taking it all in. Some women seemed to think they were doing themselves a disservice if they did not find cause for complaint.

But Julie Wimpole was satisfied. The sitting-room did not indicate much artistic taste: cheap and insensitive prints of autumnal woodland scenes and a hotch-potch of bric-à-brac; but she did not betray any opinion.

'I think the weather will clear. We're well placed for some lovely walks: Castleton, Eldon Hill, or if you're not feeling all that energetic, a gentle amble about our own fields.'

That was as near as Anne Bagshaw came to pumping Julie about her intentions of spending her time. Julie told her nothing.

'Don't worry about me. I shall be fine. I'm never bored.'

Then she had a moment's difficulty with her vocal chords.

'There's just one thing, Mrs Bagshaw. I said a fortnight, but I wonder if we could come to some agreement about an extra night? That's two weeks today – the Friday?'

'I'm afraid that won't be possible. I have another letting, the very day you go.'

Julie was disappointed.

'I'm sorry, but I couldn't possibly put him off. He's staying until Easter.'

'Pity: I mean, not for him, for me.'

But she still looked put out.

'I would normally be able to offer you another of our letting-rooms, but my husband has just stripped everything down for rewiring.'

'I expect I'll find something. Do they let rooms in the village pub?'

'They do, but they're often fully booked at weekends, even in winter. I wouldn't lose any time, if I were you. Would you like me to give them a ring for you?'

'Oh, would you, please?'

But where is the evidence for any of this? I can only make the excuse that this is all Kenworthy's influence. That is the way his mind carries him, and the way he insisted my mind must carry me. There is no failure, he repeated twice a day, except failure of the imagination.

'Who said that, Shiner?'

'Dunno, sir. You did.'

25

'Charles Morgan.'

Kenworthy wove ceaseless fantasies about any clue that we found, and brow-beat me to romanticise with him. In all fairness, his reading of events was often remarkably exact. It was better to be wrong occasionally than never right, he said.

It was Julie Wimpole's insistence on that fifteenth night that put Anne Bagshaw on to the thought that she was here to get married.

'And who, Shiner,' Kenworthy asked me, 'in this day and age has need of the vestry register in Peak Low? I'd have thought we'd made marriage easy enough by now for anyone who isn't actually contemplating bigamy, incest or baby-snatching.'

'I can't think, off-hand,' I said. 'There may be circumstances . . .'

The fact was that Peak Forest and Peak Low had taken us by surprise. We had never heard of them. The venue had never had the popularity of Gretna Green. Maybe, in spite of that vicar of the 1930s, the anvil was more of a draw than the altar.

'It's only fifteen days' residence in Peak Low,' I said. 'In Scotland it's twenty-one. You could save a week by coming to Derbyshire. And Gretna Green isn't a church ceremony – only a promise in front of a secular witness.'

All the same, there had been very few recent 'foreign' marriages in Peak Low.

'She must have been an incorrigible romantic,' Kenworthy said. 'That's if that's really why she came here. Do *you* believe it, Shiner?'

'Everybody else seems to.'

'Ah, then, that clinches it. How could a majority ever be wrong? Let's put all our future cases to the popular vote, shall we?'

In fact, Anne Bagshaw had had no doubts at all

about Julie Wimpole's intentions, yet no grounds for belief other than the urgency of that extra night within the parish bounds. About the Peak Low cross-roads, the certainty was equally apparent. A woman shopper in the Post Office–General Store had asked Julie outright when they could expect to see her boy-friend. And when she went into the Three Horseshoes to confirm her reservation for the fifteenth night, she had to run the gauntlet of voices raised unnaturally for her benefit.

'He hasn't turned up yet, then, Miss?'

She choked a little, but looked at them with satirical abandon.

'No. And until he does, I'm still considering better offers.'

'There's a chance for Will Beard yet, then?'

Will was not amongst those present. But she affected not to hear this, and no one followed it up.

And the drinkers' attitude to Julie Wimpole was beginning to harden. They had shades of uncertainty about her. She was showing lines of curiosity that were to touch some sensitive spots in Peak Low.

CHAPTER FOUR

She had woken early on her first morning at Starvelings, come down the stairs and let herself into the farm-yard whilst dawn was still a tenuous grey and the twigs of brittle trees were still sheathed in rime.

Nothing need surprise us about that, Kenworthy said. She was, if not within the strict meaning of the term, on holiday, obviously a professional woman with leisure untypically on her hands. What was more natural than, being awake, she should be impatient to visit the focal point of her pilgrimage? The locality evidently meant something to her and, having arrived under cover of darkness, she had seen nothing of it yet. She let herself out of the yard, sensible warm slacks this morning, a woollen ski-ing cap, a vivacious blue wind-cheater, the metal gate-fastenings burning cold through the palms of her gloves – trust Kenworthy to think of adding that kind of detail. She went down the sheep-track up which she had climbed with Will Beard, crossed the hoar-sprinkled plank bridge at Drydale Head, and then made a whimsical bee-line for the spot at which she was ultimately to meet her death. There was a triple irony in that.

We had no difficulty in finding witnesses of her movements. In those bare hills and folds of sparsely wooded valley it is often an illusion to imagine oneself solitary and unobserved. It is easy for a native, knowing the terrain, to keep an unobtrusive eye on the comings and goings of a stranger. David Bagshaw, for example, saw her round the crack of his cow-shed door, as he measured out the day's ration of concentrates. One of the Bagshaw children watched her through a scratch in the white paint of a lavatory window. A shot-firer on his way to the Quarries over a sky-line ridge saw her pause on the bridge, throw a fallen leaf into the Drydale brook and stand to watch the current snatch it round the stones. Then she turned and began to walk down the valley.

Thus to the spot at which she was destined to die – but not today, not this week, even. It was a corner not only tailor-made for murder but already twice in-famous for it. I have called her fate a triple irony, but

28

this would be fair comment only if it had been fortuitous. Our only safe assumption was that she went there because of something that she knew.

Among the papers which the local C.I.D. had made over to us was a pamphlet privately printed by an amateur historian – he signed himself, cryptically, *Mantillus* – more notable for his racy style than for his proof-reading. It was an account, imaginatively expanding oral traditions, of a crime that had taken place in these backwoods about two centuries ago to this very year.

1758 – the date itself was significant: the first official attempt had now been made to reduce the spate of runaway marriages, and these had dwindled to a mere trickle. Any couple who arrived now in Peak Low with the evident intention of keeping fifteen nights must obviously have been the centre of more than passing interest. It might scarcely have been true to say that all Peak Low loved an eloping couple; but for a moment all Peak Low stopped what it was doing to look.

The man was taciturn, to judge from his clothes hailed from a milieu of some quality: new leather riding boots that creaked as he walked, silk flounces at his cuffs and a velvet tricorn hat from which he flicked the dust when he took it off in the inn. He gave his name as Walter Chapman, which nobody believed, though no one in that inn was offended by robust deceit. He was a well-built figure, with eyes that did not smile when his mouth did, and he had the sort of chin that looked as if it welcomed challenges.

The girl, on the other hand, had a touch of subdued gaiety about her which it would obviously not take very much to liberate. Clearly she had been disciplined to look nothing but demure whilst her escort was negotiating with the landlord. But as she stood half a pace behind him while this talk was going on, it was not difficult for her to catch the eyes of some of the silent men who were sitting round the walls of the room.

Walter Chapman stayed for one night in the Three Horseshoes, and so did Mary Boothroyd. The next day, Chapman followed up enquiries he had made and took her up into the hills to the cottage of one Kitty Staden, a widow, and something it seemed of an enigma in the village. Having seen her installed in a tiny bedroom overlooking a slope of Drydale, Chapman rode away, having let it be clear that he would be back again to claim his own in two weeks' time. It seems probable that he paid Kitty Staden well for her stewardship, for Mary Boothroyd was so well guarded that the village did not see anything of her for the first week. Then a few of the more restless habitués of the Horseshoes, reminding each other of her come-hither smile, had ridden out, well fortified, to test out their theories. It seems that the wish to outwit Kitty Staden was a strong tonic to their enthusiasm.

They did not, however, achieve anything but blood on their boots. Long before they reached the cottage, they maintained, they found the body of the girl, her head stove-in under a fifty-six-pound boulder, lying against the ruins of an old shepherd's hut in one of the lonelier twists of Drydale. They then rode frantically up to the cottage, to find Kitty Staden in the grotesque act of trying on some of the trousseau that Mary Boothroyd had brought with her in her pack.

That was the men's story, but it was not, of course, believed. They did their best to throw suspicion on to Kitty Staden, and for some time the popular choice of culprit alternated between them and her. Justice was ultimately achieved by means of a compromise: the whole bunch of them, men and woman too, were hanged before an appreciative crowd, one crisp and quickening autumn day in the heart of the county town. Some fifteen years later a naval officer called Devereux, dying of grape-shot on the poop of Cornwallis's flag-ship off Yorktown, was said to have confessed to the chaplain of the fleet that in his youth he had posed as one Chapman – and had stolen back to Peak Low before the end of his fortnight to rid himself of an incubus.

The amateur historian left a great deal of essential detail unexplained. It is difficult enough, even at the height of the twentieth century, to get hold of trial transcripts, and there was no possibility of retrieving the legal arguments of the 1750s. Even the time and date of the trial were not established, and *Mantillus* had made no attempt to explain how Devereux-Chapman had managed to coax his victim away from Kitty Staden's without the old woman's knowledge. Nor had he made anything of the coincidence that he should have done so at precisely the hour when the pack from the Horseshoes was on the prowl. But there was evidence for the execution in the facsimile of a street ballad, allegedly a confession by concerted voices.

Kenworthy and I went down to the scene of the crime, as desolate a spot as even that forsaken valley has to offer. It was forsaken in that the narrow path that meandered in its depth led from nowhere to nowhere and was used only by the occasional labourer who had business between one farm and the next. The valley was named Drydale because there were subterranean waterswallows in the porous limestone that absorbed the brook in all but the wettest seasons. Consequently one could stand with the rushing of this tortured watercourse in one's ears, and yet not be able to see it. And the banks and valley floor were strewn with the terminal litter of a primeval glacier, steep chutes of fist-sized scree and huge slabs of rock weighing several tons each, which nothing short of blasting could shift.

It was from conveniently shaped lumps of this debris that the ancient shepherd's shelter had been fashioned, though when it had fallen into disrepair was a matter for conjecture. It was unquestioned that it was already a ruin when Mary Boothroyd met her end, her skull shattered by one of its larger stones, held for one terrifying second high above her assailant's head before he brought it down between her eyes. It was in fact probable that the rock that had been used might still be amongst those strewing the ground as we poked about in the foundations of the ruin. Two hundred years of cold rain can get rid of a lot of blood.

And it was here that Julie Wimpole had come before breakfast on her first morning at Starvelings. As seemed always to have been the case with her movements, she had been observed all the way. Even in such an abandoned corner, there was no privacy. A labourer with an errand elsewhere had chosen this very day to be afoot, and had been uprooted by the county inspector who had assiduously collated much arcane information whilst Kenworthy and I were still on our way by British Rail.

Arthur Rousell had been on his way to Peak Dale, carrying over his shoulder the singletrees and draught chains of a harrow that needed blacksmith's attention. His route had brought him across Drydale at one of its shallower undulations, and he had been some fifty yards behind Julie when she first came in sight of the ruin. A striking figure by any consideration in her blue windcheater and gay woollen cap, her behaviour now so fascinated him that he stood stock-still for a full half-minute and watched.

She approached the spot as if she were afraid of it – as if, though it was now full daylight, it was into some darkened room that she was walking, with a candle that might gutter out at any second. (The simile is undiluted Kenworthy; any comment from me would be superfluous.) She stopped in her paces and looked all round herself, as if she were afraid of being seen. She must surely have looked directly at Arthur Rousell, and yet she did not appear to have seen him. Perhaps she was as utterly distracted as Rousell seemed to think; Kenworthy believed that as he would be dressed in neutral colours he had only to remain quite still to go undetected. At any rate, she stood back for some seconds and looked at the ruin, then followed the example of most visitors to this place: advanced, climbed on to a slab of fallen lintel, and looked through the vestigial doorway at the rubble within.

As far as could be seen, the hut had consisted of a single small square room, now a mere tumble of limestone, through which protruded the frost-bitten stalks of the year's crop of nettles. She made as if to climb inside, but there was obviously nothing there that could not be seen from where she stood, and after a moment's contemplation she stepped back off the slab. Then she looked idly about her, casually picked up a stone that had fallen from one of the walls, turned it over in her hands – and suddenly flung it away as if it disgusted her.

Kenworthy himself went through her actions exactly as Rousell had described them, even to the extent of stooping to pick up a stone, which he solemnly examined as if he were confident that it was the one she had handled. As if he had been oblivious of my presence, he then cast it down with a theatrical little yelp of horror. Then he noticed me again and beckoned me to come with him round to the southern side of the pile.

It was here that Julie Wimpole had been killed. Kenworthy brought out the photographs of the lie of the body and examined the site from all angles without finding anything worthy of remark. She too had had her head smashed in by an uplifted stone. There were still stains and spatterings here and there on the wrecked walls. We looked carefully round for anything of interest that the local force might have missed, but found nothing. The stone that had been used as a weapon in this case had been taken to headquarters, where it had so far proved unproductive.

'Mad?' Kenworthy asked, and like so many of his sudden questions it left me stupidly inarticulate.

'I mean, Shiner, *was* she mad? Did she *know* she was coming here to be killed? Did she *want* to be killed? Is there really such a thing as a death-wish, that suddenly predominates when the mind goes out of gear? It's a second carbon copy – with divergences, of course, but similar enough for someone to have meant it as a copy. She must have known about at least one of the previous incidents, otherwise she'd not have come down here and behaved like that. But surely she can't have helped to plan her own death? It does look ludicrously as if she connived in the stage-management of it.'

'A strange woman, certainly.'

Kenworthy seemed to have me so mesmerised that I had become incapable of saying anything that was not banal.

'Well – this morning's papers ought to stir someone's memory. I hope today will not be too far advanced before someone comes forward and tells us who she was.'

The smashing in of her face had not left us in a position to publish a photograph. We were relying on an artist's impression; and the man who had sat in the mortuary to sketch that was a hero of a kind.

Julie had cast aside the stone with loathing, had taken a final look at the ruin and then walked briskly back up the dale to eat a breakfast that Anne Bagshaw had cooked for her, since she had not yet had the opportunity to lay in her own provisions. This she did at the General Store later in the morning, and had then kept to her flat until the evening. This Kenworthy did not find either surprising or sinister; he gave it the full treatment.

'You can picture her, Shiner: a professional woman, we're already pretty sure of that. Probably a perpetual exile in bed-sitter-land, in some northern city, if not in Manchester itself. So here she is suddenly with space of her own – her own cooker, her own pots and pans, her own fridge – the right to call them her own for a few days, anyway. *Housewives' Choice* and *Woman's Hour* ad lib. God, a woman like that could get a hell of a kick out of cooking herself even a single meal at leisure; of being able to do for a few hours the very things that most women would give their ears to get away from.'

'She'd have got an even bigger kick,' I said, 'from cooking a meal with wine and candle-light for a guest.'

'Yes, well, if she was really waiting for the arrival of the groom, she'd have chance to rehearse that as well. I don't see any inconsistencies so far, Shiner.'

He was in no hurry to leave the surrounds of the shepherd's hovel, though they were clearly going to yield nothing of practical use to us. He began to walk round the ruin a second time.

'I'm thinking about the second murder, this time, Shiner.'

35

He was play-acting now. Sometimes I thought he was deliberately trying to exasperate me. He approached the gap of the doorway again and repeated all the actions that he had performed not five minutes previously: climbing on to the lintel, picking up the stone, casting it aside, walking round again to the blood-spattered southern aspect.

'Come on, Shiner. You do the same. But fill your mind with 1940 this time. Forget about Mary Boothroyd and Julie Wimpole. Take a gander at things from the point of view of Sally Mason.'

It was in the sunny spring of Dunkirk year that the first carbon copy murder had been perpetrated. Sally Mason was an elegant, quiet, pale and potentially interesting girl who had revealed nothing whatever about herself to the village. Like Mary Boothroyd nearly two hundred years before her time, she had been brought here by a man who knew his own mind – and who reserved his background to himself. He was a second lieutenant of Royal Artillery, newly gazetted from the appearance of his uniform: service dress, Sam Browne, and a lanyard under his left epaulette, all looking as if they were fresh from his outfitter's cutting-table. Like the eighteenth-century couple, they spent one night at the Three Horseshoes, keeping themselves strictly to their separate rooms at night. On this the evidence of the landlord and his servants was adamant. Like Mary Boothroyd, Sally Mason was then moved over to an outskirt cottage, though not the household of an eccentric virago in the mould of Kitty Staden. Her landlady was a sober, God-fearing daughter of the village whose husband was driving an army lorry in Belgium. We were able to talk to Mrs Ada Bramwell ourselves, and she remembered the events of seventeen years ago as if they had been yesterday – for, in fact, she had been constantly renewing them in her mind ever since. Sally Mason was a nice girl, the sort of daughter that a woman like Ada Bramwell would like to have had. But she volunteered nothing about herself. Not rudely, for there was about her a certain quality that made rudeness unthinkable, she let it be known that their relationship could be nothing but pleasant, as long as it was understood that no questions were to be asked. And nor were they, Mrs Bramwell insisted, not even indirectly. Now and then Sally Mason showed herself a fluent talker, one indeed whose frankness had been unnaturally bottled up. And suddenly, reminiscing about her pets, or her books, or her father's enslavement to his garden, she would almost trip over the verge and say too much, remember herself with a blush – and go off to find something to do in the safety of solitude. She never did reveal where she lived, or who her family were – or who was the man who would be returning to marry her without banns. It was tacitly understood that her purpose was to defeat parental opposition, but that it was part of her philosophy at all costs to be married in a church. With all of which Mrs Bramwell happily sympathised, as being the stuff of the proper poetry of life.

Sally Mason spent most of her abundant spare time that fortnight taking easy walks in the immediately surrounding hills. She was a stranger to Derbyshire and there was much that attracted her, under ideal weather conditions. She answered courteously all who talked to her, which seems to have been practically everybody about the village and farms, but on balance they learned even less about her than Ada Bramwell had. There were some troops, an Anti-Aircraft Battery, quartered in a field along the Peak Forest road, and they seemed to have done a fair amount of bantering when she passed their encampment, teasing her and trying to date her, and pressing her to go to their Saturday night dance in the village hall. There was nothing very serious about this; she blushed so readily that she was fair game for harmless fun. Certainly she gave them no encouragement and indeed after two such encounters began to give the camp a wide berth.

Her subaltern was due to appear on her second Saturday, but on the Friday she left Mrs Bramwell's house early in the morning – for no reason that was ever brought to light – and was not again seen alive. Her body, her head savagely battered, was found against the wall of the Drydale hulk. In the long wet grass not far away was found a large pocket knife, complete with cavalryman's bodger, of the type that was still a general issue at that time to the Gunners.

The second lieutenant did not return. The moment the press had her name, Sally Mason's bewildered parents came forward at Godalming. They knew nothing of their daughter's love-life. Description of the man brought no response: he was an archetypal figure. Several hundred of his sort had been commissioned since the beginning of the war, and at least a third of these were already dead in Norway or France, or prisoners of war in Eastern Germany and beyond. Six men of the Ack-ack battery could not produce their knives at a kit inspection; but each of them had an alibi. So this time nobody was hanged.

'And why does a man,' Kenworthy asked, 'want to commit a carbon copy murder in the first instance? Either because he's a bloody artist of a peculiar kind or, if he's sane, because he wants to confuse the issue. Which, we've got to admit, he's succeeded in so far. One odd thing about all three cases, Shiner – ?'

'Why the devil did each of those women go down to Drydale anyway?'

'Well done, Shiner. I am tempted to keep you on. That is an aspect to which I propose to apply some significant effort, leaving you to get on with what I am sure you will consider all the real work. And what is more, I've got a sneaking idea that 1940 is going to be easier to unearth than 1957.'

'There can't possibly be a connection,' I said. 'Julie Wimpole can't have been more than fourteen or fifteen at the time.'

'Splendid, Shiner. I could hardly have hoped for a mathematician into the bargain. That, my son, is the conclusion I had come to myself. And that is where *I* see a link.'

'You're going too fast for me.'

'But what I want to know is, why now?'

'*Why now?*'

'Why did Julie Wimpole choose now to come and dig it all up again?'

'You think – ?'

'I don't think anything yet, Shiner. You really must not allow your imagination to carry you away. One thing you may be relieved to know: I don't propose to bother my head too much about what happened in 1758. Though if we can clear that up while we're about it, it won't do our reputation any harm.'

CHAPTER FIVE

There had been other items of anomalous behaviour, too – odd things that Julie Wimpole had done, in and around Peak Low, that had an irrational aura about them, although she had always behaved with the aplomb of a woman who knew what she was about. I was convinced that here were things that had to be followed up, that must surely merge into some indicative pattern. It was clearly the opinion too of the people who had troubled to report all this to us. But Kenworthy was more inclined to deflate us all than to be roused himself. He said that you could make out a case that ninety people out of a hundred were round the bend, if that was what you wanted to prove. Follow a man a hundred and fifty yards along a street, taking note of all his subtle changes of pace, the things he stops to read and look at in shop windows, the twists and twirls of his private superstitions, and you could make a guilty drop-out out of everyone you came across.

There had been, for example, Miss Wimpole's first visit to the Three Horseshoes – the time she had gone, successfully, to confirm her booking of that room for the fifteenth night. She had gone in shortly after opening time on her first day, had naturally entered the lounge Bar. There were two men in there, Cantrell and one other. Their cars were parked in the forecourt, and they were clearly having a habitual quick one before going home from work. Julie Wimpole caught sight of them and changed her mind, turned in the open door and went instead into the public bar, even though there were eight or nine rough and ready types in

there, with whom she was presently bandying chaff –
and in front of whom she had to conduct the suggestive
business of booking the room. Why?

'To avoid Cantrell,' I suggested, 'having already
pigeon-holed him as a kerb-crawler, and preferring a
bout of knockabout vulgarity to his peculiar style.'

'Perhaps,' Kenworthy said, in a tone that suggested
he was round three or four further corners already.

'What else, then?'

'I can't help thinking, Shiner, from what we've put
together about Julie Wimpole so far, that she was not
only pre-eminently capable of putting Cantrell in his
place if she'd wanted to, but that she would have taken
extreme pleasure in doing so.'

'So what's your reading, sir?'

'It was the other man she wanted to avoid.'

'You think she knew him too?'

'Obviously.'

'How could she have known him?'

'I would have thought that that was pretty obvious
by now, too,' Kenworthy said sourly. I was beginning
to wish myself five hundred miles from him. When it
came to deduction, I believed that he would have put
his money on the most ludicrous of outside chances,
for the sake of play-acting in front of a shackled junior.

Julie had stayed for about an hour in the public bar,
drinking one gin and tonic, which she insisted on paying for for herself, in spite of generous pressure. She had
talked – there had been no stopping her, men had had
to listen and join in – about politics and skiffle, tele-
vision comics, the Motor Show and juvenile delinquents. She had left behind about as confused a picture
of herself as I had by now formed of Kenworthy.

Roughly every other day she had gone into the Three
Horseshoes, and always the pattern was the same. She

stayed about an hour, refused to be treated, took only one drink – twice it had been half a pint of draught bitter – and talked to all comers on all subjects under the sun. Always her conversation was original and provocative, informed on current fashions from pop to painting, veering towards intellectual left wing, but strenuously denying party membership of any kind. She took a mischievous pleasure in irritating reactionaries, well represented in the Shoes. Most of them thought she was wrong about most things, but they were tickled at the pebbles that she slung at some of the tribal giants. When she missed a visit, they clearly missed her.

On the morning of her second Sunday she had gone into the pub a few minutes after midday and found it a good deal more busy than usual, thanks to the weekend influx of fell-walkers, family motorists and villagers indulging themselves. She bought herself a gin, having first found herself a gap between rugger players' elbows at the counter. What was now accepted as her circle was equally disorganised by the crush, and she had not been able to convene her usual debating society, now known in its own ranks as the Shadow Cabinet. She carried her drink away from the bar and it was at this point that another group came in, half a dozen young people in anoraks and studded boots, who had arrived impossibly packed into a Standard Eight which had been crazily painted in the manner which we would nowadays call psychedelic. They came in noisily, oblivious of anyone in the room except themselves, and burrowed themselves a space at the counter.

No one could swear to the moment of Julie Wimpole's going, but it was noticed very shortly after the new arrivals that she was no longer there, and that she had left her drink, barely touched, on the corner of a table already loaded with bottles and glasses. I started asking questions hoping to unearth the identity, or at least the provenance, of these hill-rambling extroverts. Had anyone noticed which way they had driven off? Had they dropped any names? Any hints as to their hometown? Had they spoken with an identifiable accent? Were they a works party? Or from a college? Had anyone, by unlikely chance, cast an eye on their registration plates?

Hopeless. And Kenworthy must have been convinced from the beginning that it would be, for he merely looked on while I tried, rather like an idle spectator watching a small boy try to fly a kite on a windless day.

'She was anxious to avoid being spotted by them,' I said.

'Very likely, Shiner.'

'That's why I thought it worth while – '

'I know. But if they'd known anything, they'd have told us, without being asked. And as the self-same information will be coming to us from another quarter in the next hour or so, it's hardly worth risking brain fatigue.'

Julie Wimpole's other piece of curious behaviour had begun in the Post Office. She had gone in for stamps and asked, almost as an afterthought, if they kept a copy of the Electoral Roll. They produced it for her and she stood and studied it on the spot, though not in such a way as to give an inkling as to which page it was that interested her. There were something between four and five hundred names on the printed sheets, and she appeared to find the one she wanted without trouble, and handed the list back almost at once. But she had allowed her eye to rest at two or three points in the document, as if she definitely did not want people in the shop to know whom she was looking for. And this

43

seemed to me to fall in very nicely with the general picture. As I said to a wholly unimpressed Kenworthy, if she had badly wanted to know the whereabouts of anyone in Peak Low, she had only to ask the Bagshaws. Therefore this was something that she wanted to keep from even their notice.

Having found what she apparently wanted to find, she walked at once out of the village, with the calculatedly casual gait of a woman who wishes it to be known that she is lingering with idle interest over everything she encounters. She made her way along a farm-track obliquely uphill from the main cross-roads. She was not being watched fortuitously now, but keenly, and was seen to break into a brisk pace as soon as she was away from the hub of the village. She knew where she was going; but she did not actually arrive anywhere. The lane – from the state of its ruts it looked as if it was not used more than once or twice a week – disappeared from general view for some yards behind a shippon, emerged again to partial observation behind a sparse plantation of sycamores, then wound round the almost windowless rear of a farm over a steep rise, from which it commanded a view of a single row of some five or six terraced stone cottages. And this was as far as she went – not to the cottages themselves, but to a point from which she could look down on them. This she did, and whatever she saw – no one offered us even optimistic speculation on the point – was enough to change her mind for her, decisively and without loitering. She came back along the lane very briskly indeed, and went back through as much of the village as was necessary to bring her back to Starvelings with the minimum of hindrance. She did not appear in Peak Low again that day.

Kenworthy refused to admit to the slightest flutter

of excitement. But within minutes of hearing this report, we were in the tracks that she had trodden. He got up lazily and we sauntered over to the Post Office. Kenworthy asked for the Voters' List and flicked over its pages as inconsequentially as Julie Wimpole was said to have done. Then he handed it to me and I did the same. I did not see that we could possibly glean any practical information, and I saw no point at all in yet another superficial imitation of Julie's movements. But he was clearly bent on a thorough repetition of events. We went to the cross-roads and up the rising track, past the shippon and behind the farm, skirting the autumn-stripped huddle of trees, and so reached the spot from which Julie Wimpole had turned back.

Kenworthy leaned on the coping of the wall and looked, as she had done, down on Stedman's Cottages. There were half a dozen of them, and I could not put a date to their architecture, for they were of that grey local stone which does no more than echo the ageless-ness of its mother hillside. Later – not that it matters – we were to establish that they had been put up by some paternalist developer in the late eighteenth century to house the workers in a newly opened quarry.

Unlike Julie Wimpole, we did not retrace our steps.

'Got it?' Kenworthy asked.

'Got what, sir?'

He swore like a watch-dog snarling in half sleep and volunteered no more. We walked past the first of the cottages. A child of pre-school age was playing a com-plex fantasy involving two rag dolls, a broken red tricycle and an even more decrepit tin pram. She fled at our approach, leaving her toys scattered under our feet; but not, I think, in fear. I was sure she had rushed indoors to report strangers. This three-year-old was already well schooled in the Peak Low scouting tradition.

But it was not to her house that we were going. Kenworthy led me confidently up to a door in the middle of the row, on which he rapped with his knuckles. There was no knocker, no bell-push, not even a letter-box. Peak Low set store by the privacy of the individual.

A woman opened to us – a woman in her mid-thirties, healthy-looking, as was common in an area second to none for the freshness of its air. She looked well fed and was just beginning to put on a little comfortable weight. Her hair was hidden under a printed cotton kerchief, considerably faded, and in her hand the nozzle of a vacuum cleaner was pointed at us like a futuristic weapon at the end of its flexible tube.

'Mrs Annie Broomhead?'

She nodded nervously. Her eyes raked our faces in turn.

'You know who we are – or, at least, I would think you do. But we'd better reassure you. May we come in?'

He was already in and had brought out his wallet. She barely looked at our warrant cards, as if we might be insulted if she doubted our identity.

'You've been expecting us?'

She did not answer, covered her uneasiness by dismantling her cleaner and stowing its components in a cupboard under the stairs.

'You jolly well ought to have been,' Kenworthy said. 'You must have known – '

It was a cosy room, over-furnished in a variety of styles. Arm-chairs and settee were of cheap inter-war fashion, table and dining-chairs the pride of the previous generation. A walnut-veneered sideboard was immediate post-war utility, already beginning to look

46

far from new, and the general dearth of space was accentuated by a domineering upright piano, the pages of a child's album open on the music-rest.

'Mr Kenworthy, there's no way in which I can possibly help you. I haven't seen Julie – '

'Since the early years of the war,' Kenworthy supplied.

'Since 1941. The school packed up, you know, for lack of funds. So many of the parents were taking their children back to London. And the Principals hadn't been used to running a boarding-house. They made an awful mess of the catering.'

She made a wry face in memory.

'Well, there's one way in which you can help us for a start. We only know her as Julie Wimpole.'

'And I never knew her married name. To me she was always Julie Patterson.'

'You've corresponded with her ever since?'

'Hardly ever. She wrote in 1942, when she was getting married. A whirlwind engagement. She was beside herself. So young, so unexpected – and so like Julie.'

'And since then?'

'Not at all.'

'Yet she was coming to see you.'

She looked as if she wanted to deny it, but her blush and confusion made it impossible for her to be a downright liar.

'Now come along, Mrs Broomhead, don't try to mess us about. We haven't the time, and you wouldn't have the staying power.'

'She *didn't* come, Mr Kenworthy.'

'But you saw her?'

'I was shaking a mat, and I saw her up along the lane. She saw me too, I know that, but she didn't make

47

a sign. She turned on her heel, and that was all I saw of her.'

'You were disappointed?'

She pouted. You couldn't have called her good-looking, or free from the harassments of post-war housewifery. But there was a certain well-founded contentment about her, excluding her anxiety of the moment. I took her for a woman who got a good deal of quiet fulfilment from her family circle.

'Why should I be disappointed? If she could not be bothered – '

'You mean, the sight of you reminded her that she was a cut above you?'

'Nothing of the sort. There was nothing of that about Julie. The opposite, in fact.'

'What, then?'

'She just couldn't be bothered, I suppose. She spotted me and had second thoughts. But it wouldn't have been because she felt superior.'

There was a weakness here in which I expected Kenworthy to start probing at once; but I was unused as yet to his habit in interrogation. He liked to act as if he had all the time in the world, and he was adept at appearing to miss crucial points. His next smile was meant to put Mrs Broomhead at her ease.

'You sound to me like a local girl.'

'As local as the Three Horseshoes.'

'So how come you were at school at the Powder Mill?'

'When they first came here, they were glad to take on a few day-girls. It all helped to balance the books. And my parents were all for it. They thought that the southerners would pass on a bit of their polish.'

'And did they?'

'Not that you'd notice. They made me take elocution lessons.'

'Did many village girls enrol?'

'Only three of us – '

She shook her head, knowing where Kenworthy was leading.

'The other two left the district ages ago.'

'And you were Julie Patterson's special friend?'

'I wouldn't say that.'

'Though she sought you out last week? Or nearly did?'

'We were friends. Julie was like that. That's what I meant just now when I said there was no snobbery in her. It wasn't all that easy for the likes of me, coming into that sort of circle, with all their cliques and friendships neatly sewn up. But Julie didn't give two hoots for the established order. She wanted a friend in the village.'

'Which you became?'

'You could say that. She had an independent mind. She wanted a jumping-off spot in the village, that she could use for her own little ventures. She used to come to tea with us on Sundays – by special permission.'

'She was an unusual sort of girl, you'd say?'

'Very unusual.'

I, and practically every other member of the squad, would have followed that up. But Kenworthy, seeing something air-borne, always seemed to want to get another ball off the ground without delay.

'And all this was in the spring of Dunkirk?'

'They'd come here in 1939. The first week in September. But they were still here at the time of Dunkirk.'

'So she caught sight of you last week, saw into your domesticity, and decided not to draw you back into things?'

This was vision; and she did not like it. The stillness

of her hands in her lap came from sheer determination not to fidget.

'Something else happened that spring, besides the evacuation in the Little Ships, Mrs Broomhead.'

'You mean – ?'

'You know very well what I mean. You tell me. Volunteer something for a change.'

'You mean that girl – '

She looked hopefully to Kenworthy to help her out; but he wasn't playing.

'The girl who was murdered in Drydale? The one who was waiting for the officer? Is that what you mean?'

'What else? It must have caused quite a stir in your little school.'

'We talked about it, certainly.'

'Before she was killed, I mean.'

She made an effort that she must have known was pitifully doomed to failure.

'Now, Mr Kenworthy, how could we have talked about it before it happened?'

'You are not trying to tell me, Mrs Broomhead, that a community of adolescent girls, with three of you coming in daily with all the news from the village, was not agog about a runaway marriage. Did anybody talk about anything else, I wonder?'

'We did talk about it, yes.'

'Especially Julie Patterson?'

'Not Julie more than any other of us.'

'No? Yet she was an inquisitive child. Tell me, Mrs Broomhead, had you, or any of your friends, actually met this bride-in-waiting? I had her name on the tip of my tongue – '

'Sally Mason.'

'Yes, I thought you'd remember. You'd met her, had you?'

50

'Yes, we had met her.'

'All of you? Some crocodile, botanising in the hills?'

'Not a crocodile, Mr Kenworthy. A few of us out on a ramble.'

Annie Broomhead started to cry – a smarting tear at first, then a spasm of sobbing which it took her a minute or two to master. Kenworthy sat smiling kindly.

'I'm sorry,' she said at last.

'No need to be sorry. You've a lot on your mind, and it's been there a long time.'

'Neither Julie nor I did anything wrong, Mr Kenworthy.'

'I would be very surprised if you had. But I need to know all about it. You know that, surely. I need a full statement. In writing. In your own words. Collect yourself and begin at the beginning. Leave nothing out, because there's always the possibility that I might know more than you think. I'll call again this evening.'

When he got us outside again, he was more expansive, more restful, it seemed, than he had been at any time since we had left London.

'You didn't get it, Shiner.'

'No, sir – if you mean what led you to Annie Broomhead.'

'*Annie*, Shiner. If there hadn't been an unusual Christian name in the franchise, I'd have been scuppered. The school was a reasonably safe gamble. There wasn't much else that could account for a woman of Julie's age, unknown to the villagers, having a partially forgotten knowledge of a hole like this: given that there was a school, and that the Keelings, of whom she spoke to Will Beard, left the place a little after the school did. So she asks for the Voters' List. She might have been looking for anyone of course, but if it was for a married

51

woman of her own age, she might not know her surname. But *Annie*, yes: not *Anne*, with or without an *e*. *Annie. Broomhead, Annie Margaret, 3, Stedman's Cottages*. It stood out a mile.'

'A long shot, sir.'

'Not as long as some I've made in my time – and failed with. But if I hadn't risked it, we'd still be nowhere. And you hadn't even brushed on it, Shiner?'

I admitted that I'd come nowhere near it.

'Well, at least you can tell me why I've left her feverishly at it with pen and paper.'

'I must confess I'd have struck while the iron was hot.'

'What iron, Shiner? You'd have given yourself away. Now I'll make an admission. I've very little idea what any of this is about. She's going to tell us. But Annie Broomhead is an intelligent woman, as well as a worried one. I only had to trip into one uninformed question, and she'd have spotted my ignorance. Then she might have started editing, and everything would have taken us longer, Shiner; we'd have been longer away from home than we're going to be as it is.'

He stopped walking. We had rounded the last bend in the track and were now within sight of the cross-roads. He picked up a stone and flung it hopelessly wide of a lapwing strutting in a stony field.

'Shiner, I don't mind telling you that you're with me here and now because your record has a few things in it that happened to catch my eye. But nothing much has caught it since we landed in this bloody dump. What's the matter with you, lad? Are you bemused?'

I muttered something about not having got my teeth into anything so far. There were times when Kenworthy could be so crushingly frank that the truth you were staring at turned into a gorgon.

'Am I cramping your style, lad?'

'You are a bit, sir.'

He aimed a kick at another stone, which went off his toe-cap at a futile angle.

'Time I cut the umbilical cord, then. I've got a few routine things that I want to get on with. Go up to Starvelings and talk to the present lodger, the historian. Anything he can tell you about the background of these lunatics might be grist to our rollers. And use your loaf. If it looks as if it might usefully upset his apple-cart, ask him if he once wrote a pamphlet about the place and signed it *Mantillus*.'

CHAPTER SIX

We had made the brief acquaintance of Stephen Parbold on our first and only visit to Starvelings – the occasion when we had taken note of the cheap but cheerful wallpaper, when Anne Bagshaw had recalled for us the details of Julie Wimpole's arrival – and Kenworthy's imagination had assiduously accounted for everythsng else. Parbold had been working at a writing-table, in front of a litter of box-files, sheaves of manuscript and a portable typewriter: a man like several others of the personalities in this case, in his early thirties, in a roll-necked Arran sweater and baggy corduroys. There were tea-chests full of books and documents, still unpacked. The County C.I.D. had taken away Julie's personal possessions, had dusted for prints, and measured and photographed a good deal that was to prove superfluous; but they had asked

Parbold to disturb as little of the lay-out as possible until we had seen it. He had complied patiently enough, though there was a note of understandable irritation when he asked how much longer before he could spread himself. Kenworthy had pottered, rather too fussily, I thought, for a few minutes among the furniture, taken in the views from the windows, then given him the go-ahead.

I certainly had not then thought that Parbold might be an essential figure in the case, and if any such notion had occurred to Kenworthy, he had kept it uncharacteristically to himself. The man had arrived after Julie Wimpole's death. His lease of the room had been booked some months previously – and had actually redounded to Julie Wimpole's inconvenience.

If Parbold had published local legend under the pseudonym *Mantillus*, a whole new complex of possibilities unfolded. It was true that the pamphlet about the eighteenth-century murder was badly printed. But if Parbold had been its author, he could only have been a young man at the time. And such things are not unheard of: the future academic whom no power on earth can keep out of print, who had got hold of a pretty tale that had never been written up before: vanity publishing at his own expense, hoping perhaps to recoup himself by local sales to tourists.

If Parbold was *Mantillus*, things might not stop at that. I found the prospect exhilarating as I stepped out past the Powder Mill along the hill-paths to Starvelings. We already had evidence that Julie Wimpole was interested in the ancient wickedness of Drydale. She had probably, then, at some time or other, come across the *Mantillus* booklet. Could there be any closer connection? Had Julie Wimpole ever met Parbold? Was she perhaps collecting her own impressions of the murder scene to pass on to him? To *share* with him? Was there even an outside chance that she might be coming here to marry him, arriving as he did on her fifteenth day? Was that something that had to be kept sternly secret? Had she spoken about that fifteenth night within minutes of her arrival, not only because it was uppermost in her mind, but also perhaps because she wanted to draw attention away from the truth? Were the pair of them proposing to winter together in the Starvelings flat, Parbold's lease covering them until the next spring?

Kenworthy himself could not have complained about my imagination as I stood for a few seconds on the Drydale plank-bridge and, as Julie Wimpole had done, threw a leaf into the stream and watched an eddy carry it out of sight behind a smooth-licked boulder. Crazy? The thing was that however capriciously one happened upon such a theory, it became at once something that had to be exhaustively examined.

My leaf skirted the boulder, dropped into a fast little swirl of current, and then got caught up in a narrow belt of scum that had built up against the bank.

I cannot describe my sense of freedom during that walk across country. It was, of course, my release from Kenworthy that I found so stimulating. But there was another thought, too – the certainty that what had gone through my mind in the last few minutes had also gone through Kenworthy's. Maybe he had already got me consciously imitating him. But he had not troubled to feed me any help; merely dropped me the clue *Mantillus*. After that, it was sink or swim. I didn't need to be told what my future in the Murder Squad was likely to be if I chose this spot to sink.

I climbed up the sheep-track to Starvelings, determined that if ever I had my way with a man under

55

questioning it was going to be with Parbold. It was an imperative within an imperative.

Coming up within sight of the farm cluster, I was aware for the first time of footsteps behind me – lively, quick, uneven. I stopped and allowed myself to be overtaken – by two of the Bagshaw children, it being late afternoon, and they on their way home from school. They were as demonstratively glad to see me as if I had been a favourite uncle, though they had seen me only at a distance during our previous visit.

'Hey, detective! I know you. You're a detective, aren't you?'

'Have you got a gun? Hey, he's got a gun in his pocket.'

'Show us your gun, mister.'

'And your hand-cuffs.'

All a good deal less inhibited and more colloquial than would have pleased their parents; I had the feeling that the Bagshaws did their best to propagate an old-fashioned tone about their household. But these two still had the fresh air of the school playground about their ears. I told them that I had left my bracelets and my gun at home, not risking loss of face by admitting that I did not possess anything even as lethal as a starting-pistol.

'You've come here to find out who killed Miss Wimpole, haven't you?'

This was from the younger of the pair, a little girl with her hair in a pony-tail, that danced about with a life of its own when she tossed her head.

'She lived at our house.'

'Well, he knows that, stupid,' her brother said.

'I know who killed her.'

'That's stupid again, Susan, talking like that. She doesn't know anything about it, mister.'

56

'I do, then.'

'If you talk like that, you'll get taken off and have to answer questions for hours on end. Then when they find you know nothing about it – '

'I do know who killed her. It was the man who came that night.'

The boy – he would be nine or ten – blushed hotly. I waited for him to tell her that she shouldn't have said that, that she'd been told not to. But he was sharp enough to see what lay round the corner.

'We don't even know that there really was a man,' he said. 'It could have been pure imagination.'

High-sounding: it had the timbre of a parental quote. I thought I could see what had happened. A brainy, eager child, told by her parents to keep something dark, will sometimes blurt it out with an unerring instinct for the worst of wrong ears to inform. The order to keep secrets itself produces a fallacious feeling of guilt. It plays on a child's nerves. Cases have been broken that way.

'It could just have been imagination,' the lad said. 'That's why it isn't right to talk about it.'

'It wasn't imagination. We both heard it.'

We were less than fifty yards from the farm-house now. I did not want to detain the children, still less stumble into an unnecessary confrontation with the Bagshaws. I thought that perhaps there was nothing very sinister behind this, and that the parents had probably suppressed it because they believed it a fantasy. I began to walk slowly; the children still hung under my feet.

'Something you saw, was it?' I asked. 'Or heard?'

'Something we thought we heard. Something we *might* have heard.'

'I heard it, and Derek heard it, and that means we both heard it.'

'I only think I heard it.'

'That shows how you go changing your mind.'

She was angry with him because he was pin-pointing her gullibility. She suddenly charged at him with her head down and butted him in the stomach. I separated them – Susan needed more restraint than Derek – and looked down at them with my hands firmly on their shoulders.

'Now listen, you two. This probably isn't important, but sometimes it is the little things that matter most. Just tell me what you think you heard.'

I addressed myself to Derek. I thought it might be an investment to restore his dignity.

'We thought we heard footsteps on the stairs, that's all.'

'Not really footsteps, that's what we're not sure about.'

'One of the stairs creaked, and we're not certain whether it was a footstep or not. If it was somebody, he was trying not to let us hear him.'

The furnished flat had its separate staircase. Therefore if Julie Wimpole had wanted to entertain a nocturnal visitor, she might have got away with it.

'Stop a minute. When was this?'

'Late at night.'

'Which night?'

'Last Tuesday.'

'Wednesday.'

'I remember it was Tuesday. We'd had recorders at school.'

'Yes, it was. And we'd had cheese and onion pie for dinner. Yuck!'

'Didn't the dog bark?' I asked.

'Shebb barks at nothing. No one takes notice of him any more.'

'But he was barking that night?'

'We thought he smelled fox. He does sometimes.'

'I see; footsteps, perhaps – but no voices?'

'We only thought we heard voices.'

'Where?'

'In Miss Wimpole's room. It's right next to ours, but up different stairs.'

'A man's voice?'

'I wasn't sure it was a voice at all. But it wouldn't have been a woman.'

'Wouldn't it?'

'A woman wouldn't bother to have another woman in, would she?'

I did not know whether this was precocious or naive. I sent them charging indoors whilst I climbed Parbold's stairs. There was a tread about two-thirds of the way up that certainly did complain.

Parbold had by now made the flat his own. He had unpacked his chests, and through lack of space his books were stacked in vertical piles in the corners. The autumnal woodland prints had been removed and replaced by landmarks from his own life. There was no sign of any attachment to a woman: no portraits, no ornaments or gadgets that one could say at a glance were a feminine gift. It was a caricature of a bachelor apartment. Books were everywhere: over the arms of chairs, piled on the sideboard, open on the settee. He had just made tea in a brown mug. Pipe-smoke hung across the room in motionless horizontal layers. He was working from a sample-sized card-index in a cardboard carton.

'Glad to see you – Sergeant, isn't it? I was just on my way down to find you. You've saved me a walk I can well do without.'

He was built on the heavyish side, carrying a

stone too much for his age, but energetic in manner.

'She left this behind. I'm sure you ought to have it.'

He held out a paper-bound note-book, gnome and toadstools on the cover.

'She left it tucked in on the top row of the book-case. In between Vera Brittain and Zane Grey, if you want chapter and verse.'

There was something sardonic about him that I did not much like. I took the book from him and flicked over the pages. Several of them were filled, with what looked like personal memoranda in a mature but characterlessly conventional woman's hand.

'What makes you think it belonged to her?'

There was no name on or in it, no initials even.

'You can't work it out?'

He looked at me with amused satisfaction.

'Tell me,' I said.

He took the book from me and showed me the second page.

M 9 Dv 7
W Lnch Sch Sch M
F Bk

'Now what do you make of that, Sergeant? Transcript for the Russian Embassy? Or, put it another way, what did she have for lunch on Wednesday?'

'I'll obviously need a minute or two,' I said.

The best way of spoiling his fun was not to contribute to it. I turned the pages. At a quick glance there was a fair amount of stuff with a similar style of abbreviation: packing lists, shopping lists, an amateurish sketch or two, tags of poetry with words and lines missing, the omissions shown by bold dashes.

'She was a lady of parts, the previous occupant,' Parbold said. 'You're going to have fun with that little book. I can't say that I've made it all mean something, but you'll have a better grasp of her background than I have. I make no apologies for having pored over it, by the way. I didn't realise it was hers till I spotted the *M 9 Dv 7* stuff.'

So if he had indeed known her, he was starting off with a categorical disclaimer. I looked at him and tried to picture him in the role of villain, occasionally a fruitful exercise. But what does a murderer look like? Most of them would pass as abnormally normal in an average crowd. Certainly he had the physical stamina to wreak havoc with an upraised stone – but that didn't exactly single him out.

'Anything specifically about Peak Low?' I said.

'Not unless it's amongst the *esoterica*. I haven't been able to decipher all her notes. One or two rough sketches – two of the view from this window. Not all that skilled, I would say, but they may have been just notes for future work. Oddly enough, there's one of the actual spot where she was killed.'

He found it for me, a biro outline of the pile of the shepherd's hut.

'I find that strange. You might think she had an obsession with the place.'

'There are other things that point the same way,' I said.

'She certainly does seem to have had a morbid turn of mind. Look at this one.'

It was a verse couplet:

Nurse, oh my love is slain, I saw him go
Over the white Alps alone.

'You don't happen to know where that comes from?' I asked him, hoping to steal a march on Kenworthy.

'Clueless, I'm sorry. I have university colleagues who might chase it up for you.'

'I expect we'll get on to it. You're not by any

chance an expert on the Peak Low legend, are you?'

'Sorry to disappoint you, Sergeant. I'm not that kind of historian. We come in all breeds and sizes, you know. My line's industrial archaeology, which means that as far as Peak Low is concerned I can tell you about lime, gunpowder, lime, sheep-washes, lime, railway engineering – and lime. Mind you, working in the locality, and coming across this kind of yarn, one's bound to have a peep at it.'

He went to a corner pile of books and eased out something from halfway down. It was a ragged copy of the *Mantillus* pamphlet.

'The only printed record, Sergeant. And if you ask me, it's mucked up the whole issue.'

'I know it doesn't look very professional,' I started hopefully.

'Never mind about the lay-out. It's bloody bad history. He doesn't quote any of his sources. Most of his indebtedness is to a hanging ballad whose author probably wasn't beyond pulling a few facts to get his rhymes. And what's all this about a naval lieutenant who *is said to* have made a confession? Who ever said so? It isn't part of the oral tradition, I'll swear to that. So where does it come from? *Yorktown, Cornwallis* – name-dropping, scene-setters. But where did *Mantillus* find them? I mustn't pretend I've gone deeply into this. I heard the story Youth Hostelling up here before the war, and there was no naval lieutenant in it then: not that that's conclusive, I know. But I have specialist friends who feel strongly about it.'

'And you've no idea who *Mantillus* was?'

'Can't help you, I'm afraid. Local parson? Village teacher? Member of this, that or the other Parish Pump Historical Society? History is like education; every man thinks he's an expert.'

I decided to plunge.

'It's funny, you know. It's our habit to walk slowly round everything – and we did ask ourselves whether you might have been *Mantillus* yourself.'

'Very funny indeed, Sergeant. And I thought you were *Laughing P.C. Brown*. God, Sergeant – do you really think that I – '

For a man who had shown himself reasonably quick-witted during the last few minutes, he seemed remarkably slow at seeing the further implication. It came as an afterthought – but a strenuous one.

'And if you are also thinking, Sergeant, that I had some connection with the Wimpole woman, I can assure you that I never heard her name before I was told that I could only take part possession of this flat.'

I had to decide; I knew Kenworthy would ask me: I thought he was telling the truth. An intelligent man would not stick out his neck quite so far. If we now did prove a connection between him and Julie Wimpole, his position would be untenable.

As for *Mantillus*, I felt sure that his printer would help us. Printers are always sensitive about their responsibility under English law for perpetuating the work of others. But there was still this cryptic identification of the note-book itself.

'I give you best, Dr Parbold,' I said.

He enjoyed his superior moment.

    M 9 Dv 7
    W Lnch Sch Sch M
    F Bk

'Must be hers, because these were highlights of the Third Programme the first week she was here. I suppose she was going to be parted from her *Radio Times*. Dvořák's Seventh on Monday morning, Schubert's *Schöne Müllerin* in the Wednesday lunch-time concert,

Bartók on Friday. I know, because I listened to two out of the three myself.'

As I was leaving the farm, I was chased across the yard by Anne Bagshaw. She must have spent the last hour listening for my footfall on that stair.

'Mr Wright, the children have told me: I don't know what you must think of us.'

I tried to be suitably solemn without making too much of it.

'I know we ought to have mentioned it before. But the children play on each other's ideas so. It isn't that they tell us lies. They convince themselves that what they are saying is true.'

'And might indeed be true,' I said.

'In this case, I don't think so, Mr Wright.'

'Why so sure?'

'You could see she wasn't that type of woman.'

'That, Mrs Bagshaw, is about the feeblest line of reasoning I've listened to this week. Did she look like the sort of woman who might get herself killed?'

As I walked back down the sheep-track, I started lining up my report to Kenworthy. I was feeling rather less bright than when I had paused on the bridge on the way up.

CHAPTER SEVEN

I was boyishly keen to get the new evidence to Kenworthy – but I had to be patient. He was in the lounge of the Three Horseshoes with two men, one of them Cantrell, the other, I presumed the one whose presence one evening had driven Julie, Wimpole to seek more congenial company. Kenworthy waved me to a chair, made no effort to introduce me into the conversation, and screwed up his eyes when he saw me look hopefully in the direction of the bar. He did not want us interrupted.

Whatever dialogue he had been conducting with these two had devolved into an uneasy waiting silence; and it was Kenworthy who was doing the waiting. He had been screwing up the tensions; I had heard often enough of his talent for it. Cantrell and his friend were carefully looking neither at each other nor at him. Kenworthy's eyes were travelling from one to the other in turn. No one said anything, and Kenworthy was letting silence accumulate. He suddenly shifted himself in his chair.

'You're under orders to remember,' he said. 'Anything less is obstruction, and for that I shall throw the book at you.'

They were dismissed. With a touch of swagger to offset their hangdog spirit, they got up to go. Cantrell's friend was older than he was, perhaps in his mid-forties, on the over-fed side, and fairly regularly over-beered. Normally, I would have said, they were bouncingly self-satisfied men, but for the moment they were jolted. I do not know whether Kenworthy would have gone on immediately to tell me what it was all about. I forestalled him by placing Julie Wimpole's note-book in front of him. He looked at the first page, then at me, then at the first page again.

Vsts 4	*Skrts: Twd*
Knckrs 6	*Brn*
Blses 6	*Bl*
	Nyln Pttcts

There is no point in reproducing the whole list here. Each item was marked with two pencil ticks: once,

Kenworthy said, as she had piled the stuff from her wardrobe on to the bed, and once as she had checked it into her suitcase.

'One of your jobs, Shiner, will be to compare this list with what the C.I.D. are storing for us. It doesn't look, at a rough glance, does it, as if she'd anything in reserve for a formal occasion? Does this look to you like a trousseau? I wondered when we first saw the stuff. Which of this lot do you think she was planning to get married in? To my mind there's nothing much here above the neatly casual – not that that signifies too much these days, I suppose. I wish we had Elspeth here. Look at this: *Nghtdrss 3*: one on, one in the drawer, one in the wash. Better have a word with Mrs Bagshaw about what her laundry arrangements were. You'd have thought she'd have had something scanty in reserve for the wedding night, wouldn't you?'

I tried to help. 'Perhaps she didn't put it all on the list.'

'She didn't pack it, either. I made sure I looked. I'll bet Mary Boothroyd a couple of centuries ago had a better bottom drawer than this.'

Then came:

M 9 Dv 7
W Lnch Sch Sch M
F Bk

I was ready with my superior knowledge.

'Could be,' Kenworthy said.

Bkd Bns 2	*Onions*	*Pies 2*
Spgh Bol 2	*POM*	*Crnd Bf 2*
Tn Toms 1	*Knzle Cks*	*Apples 2 lb*
Pastes	*Chs Chdr*	*4 oranges*
Qkr O	*Box*	*V8 3*
Bcn	*Ambr R.P.*	*Tn Asprgs*
Mmld	*Ir St*	*Cr Crckrs*
Peas	*Spam 2*	

'Bed-sitter habits, Shiner. No flour, no fats, no cake mixtures. She wasn't dreaming up anything ambitious. Who said something about dinner for her love by candlelight? A tin of Irish stew with dehydrated spuds, followed by Ambrosia rice pudding, a triangle of processed cheese, then a toast in vegetable juices from a can?'

'Convenience foods. As you say, she's probably well accustomed to them. No butter, eggs or milk?'

'Separate list coming up, I'd think. She'd have those from the farm, wouldn't she? And her bread when Mrs Bagshaw's baker called?'

'It might be worth checking how much of this she used. Might possibly point to whether she actually entertained a guest.'

'I'll leave that to you, Shiner, since you mentioned it.'

I promised myself I'd be more careful in future.

Nurse, oh my love is slain, I saw him go
Over the white Alps alone.

'Hullo – a mountaineering friend? A hurried journey? War-time? A jilt? A winter jilt? Was she wondering whether her man would turn up or not, and trying to see how she might feel if he didn't?'

'I don't know the piece, sir. Parbold didn't, either.'

'We'd better get it to somebody with Eng. Lit. on his certificate. It might mean more to us in its proper context. One thing we can be certain of: they were evidently a couple of lines that spoke to the condition she was in. I wonder why she wrote them down. Had she just picked them up in something she'd read? Or were they something she'd remembered? Why put them in her note-book? To have them in front of her eyes? Some sort of consolation? Astringent, do you think – or merely sentimental? Something she wanted

67

to remember? But surely she did remember, so she'd no need to write them down. *Nurse, oh my love is slain* – ah, this is more concrete.'

	Mlk	Brd	Btr	Eggs		M	B	Btr	E
Sat	1	1	½	8	Sat	1			
Sun	1				Sun	1			
Mon	1	1			Mon	1	1	½	
Tue	1				Tue	1			4
Wed	1	1	½		Wed	1	1		
Thur	1			6	Thur	1			
Fri	1	1			Fri	½			

'Systematic lass. Didn't mean herself to be overcharged by Mrs Bagshaw. It looks as if she was determined to be off on the Friday – and didn't intend to leave any waste behind. She'd just about be out of commons. Bit pathetic, don't you think, ordering only half a pint of milk, just in time to go out and get killed? And if she'd been going to stay on with Parbold at Starvelings after the wedding, you'd have thought she'd have got something into the larder, wouldn't you?'

'Unless she was taking outlandish steps not to give the game away.'

'Or unless she was playing ultra-safe, because she wasn't certain he was going to turn up at all. Look at this:

Enlacing arms within this troubled sea
And in communion – – . To sleep? To wake
For aye, and in our common waking say we end
Our heart-ache and the – x – x –
That we have – x , oh aye, a consummation
Devoutly to be wished. To sleep, to dream,
Perchance a nightmare – – –

'I can't remember it all, of course, but I do know where this one comes from. Don't you, Shiner?'

I didn't; but he didn't seem to mind.

'*Hamlet*, Shiner. *To be or not to be* – that speech. The epitome of indecision – all the torment. So why should she want to put that down? Because she herself is undergoing the self-same torture; perhaps even enjoying it, who's to tell? And look, this isn't right: *Perchance a nightmare*. That isn't Shakespeare. *Perchance to dream*, that's Shakespeare, via Ivor Novello. She's chopping and changing things about.'

He sat and sank himself in the poem, and I tried to do the same, but could not keep my thoughts within the room.

'It's no good, Shiner. I can't even pretend I ever knew it – except that first line. We shall have to get hold of the full text. I thought at first that the blanks were bits that she couldn't remember. More likely they were bits that she hadn't succeeded in slotting in yet. I think she was trying to rewrite it – not exactly to parody it, but to pull it round in some way that would be more applicable to herself. Ending heart-ache for aye in a common waking – that sounds like the morning after the wedding-night: with Parbold or another. Rustle up the original words of the Bard, Shiner.'

'Yes, sir.'

'Shiner – have you ever been lonely?'

I had to think about it. I could not say that I ever really had; though some jobs had entailed a long watch or two.

'Julie Wimpole had, Shiner. I'm beginning to see quite a share of hidden depth in that lady. So lonely that she chose this way of talking to herself. Words in her head were not enough; she had to nail them down. Ah, now this is a bit more down to earth.'

69

Elecy	*G*
Ins	*LL*
Bill ⎫	*Office* ⎫
Cath ⎪	*AA* ⎪
B & S ⎬	*P* ⎬
T ⎭	*LG* ⎭

'Correspondence,' Kenworthy said. 'Holiday post-cards, but she started off by paying her electricity bill. It probably arrived just as she was leaving home, so she brought the account with her. What's *Ins*, do you reckon? *Institute*? *Insurance*? That's it: probably paying her quarterly premium. Yet we didn't find a cheque-book on her, did we? And she'd paid Mrs Bagshaw in advance by money order. Odd: she was a woman who'd have a current banking-account, surely to goodness. So what was she up to? What lengths had she thought of to try to keep her town of origin dark? Had she brought enough loose cash in her bag to cover the fifteen nights? How much had she about her, according to the C.I.D. inventory? Six quid or so? So what after that? She'd no Post Office Savings Book, no Trustee Bank pass-book. Barely enough to pay her fare back to Manchester – if Manchester it was – a meal out, and the fifteenth night here at the Horseshoes. Find out, Shiner, if she bought any postal or money orders here in the village.'

'Sir: some of those names are bracketed together.'

'Some probably got coloured cards, some black and white.'

'And it seems to me, sir, that she hadn't even a plan for herself, after that Friday morning. It's as if she knew it was all finished.'

'Yes, Shiner – finished. Or something unknown was about to begin. Now we're back with Hamlet – *a con-summation devoutly to be wished – our common waking*. I don't

70

think the poor lass knew whether she – they – were destined to wake or not. Maybe she thought she'd be tempting providence if she planned too confidently for a happy ending. Superstitious: but who isn't?'

It seemed to me that Kenworthy was turning too readily and too often back to his thesis that she didn't know whether the bridegroom was going to turn up or not. It could have been so, but I did not rate it higher than a possibility. In principle I sympathised with his imaginative excursions, was even beginning to enjoy them, but they had their dangers. Sometimes a side-valley looks so inviting that you get trapped in it. I said nothing.

He turned a page in the note-book and we came to the last two entries.

M. Boothroyd
S. Mason
J. Wimpole?

'Obsessed,' Kenworthy said. 'Absolutely obsessed. So why did she want to sit and stare at those particular words? If she was as scared as that, why did she stay?'

There are a thousand paths to the delectable tavern of death, and some run straight and some run crooked.

'Mad, Shiner? Unbalanced, to say the least? Or is this only the fever of sheer bloody solitude? What does *mad* mean, anyway? Who the hell is balanced? Obviously she spent too much time alone and thinking. She may have been an incorrigible romantic. I've said that before. But when your fantasies start coming true, including your own murder, you could be called a realist, couldn't you? This woman's beginning to grow on me, Shiner.'

He went back to the beginning of the little book and turned the pages pensively, but only found one further comment.

'One question stands out a mile, Shiner – and that's the object of her exercise. What did she know? And about whom?'

CHAPTER EIGHT

Kenworthy bought me a drink after that, and I had just begun to run over properly with him the facts of my interview with Parbold, when Mrs Broomhead walked shyly round the door, carrying a conspicuous envelope in her hand. She must have been working on her statement ever since we had visited her cottage this morning. Shabbily dressed, her outside coat dated from the war years, and had never been intended to enliven the world with a splash of colour. She seemed to think that we would want her with us while we perused her sheets. She was for lingering, but Kenworthy told her we would be in touch.

Statement by Mrs Annie Broomhead, 3 Stedman's Cottages, Peak Low, Peak Forest, Chapel-en-le-Frith, Derbyshire, concerning Julie Patterson and the Piers Plowman School in the months of April and May, 1940.

They called it the Piers Plowman School, I don't know why. For us in the village it was always the Powder Mill School. They came from somewhere in South London, Herne Hill, if I remember correctly, and had been evacuated here, a private arrangement by the Principal. She was a Miss Longhorsley and she had a partner, Miss Darwent, a cousin, I think. Miss Darwent taught very little, just a little needlework, that we all did our best to keep well away from.

In London they had been a co-educational day school, but when they came up here they left the boys behind, because the Misses Longhorsley and Darwent did not fancy a mixed boarding school. The way they organised the Powder Mill, it's perhaps as well they knew their own limitations. From the way most of the girls talked, they hadn't missed any of the opportunities of broad daylight in a busy suburb. There was only one main topic of conversation, though I took it there was more bravado than truth in most of their so-called experiences. They were too young for much else, most of them, but you could see what their minds were full of. They were a forward lot, and this was encouraged by the way the school was run. The basic idea was free discipline. We were supposed to write out our own schemes of work and go to the lessons we thought would be of most help to us. I think some of the girls got so bored that they sometimes did get their books out, but a lot of them managed to spend day after day in nothing but gossip, and the favourite *Project* was to go up into the hills on a *Regional Study*. That didn't work in bad weather, though, and 1939/40 was a terrible winter in Peak Low.

We village girls – I told you this morning, there were three of us at the school – just didn't fit in. We weren't used to this lackadaisical attitude, and the veterans of Herne Hill put up what they called a Popular Front against us. All they could talk about was their former boy-friends, whose names didn't mean anything to us, with everlasting tales of waiting-rooms on suburban railway stations where they were supposed to have got up to unmentionable capers. Not to mention a potting-shed, where I dare say a few of them might possibly have smoked a crafty

73

cigarette or two. And there had been a character called Mo who used to hang about on the pavement outside the school drive and carry betting-slips into the local pub for them – so they had spasmodic crazes for horse-racing, which wouldn't have washed in Peak Low.

Consequently, they looked upon us, and called us, the Yokels. I am going into this at some length because it seems the best way of introducing Julie Patterson. Julie was different from the rest – different, in fact, from anybody else that I have ever met. But I didn't like her at first: she seemed a busy-body, a real Nosey Parker, and scathing about the way that we lived in Peak Low. But we soon saw that she was savagely intolerant too of those that she had come up here with. Julie Patterson didn't belong to anybody. I don't know how her parents had ever managed her – maybe they hadn't. She talked very little about them, and changed the subject if ever we tried to ask questions. I suppose she talked to me about them more than anyone else, but all I gathered was that her father was some sort of arty-crafty journalist – a critic, I think – and her mother was secretary to some Top Person on Millbank, wherever that is. I gather that they left her a lot to her own devices, and she gave the impression that that was the way she liked it. Thinking about it since, I am not so sure that she did.

I eventually invited her home to tea, and she behaved a good deal better than I would have expected. Our home was quite unlike anything that Julie Patterson could ever have come across: everything going on in one room, no two pieces of furniture that matched, a gramophone with a big green horn that ought to have been in a museum, and a wireless

74

set as big as most people's sideboards that my father had made from a plan in a magazine. She asked so many questions that we all laughed at her outright. But she wasn't scornful, as she always seemed to be at school. And she was courteous to my parents – seemed to understand their difficulties, financial, social and personal, yet without drawing unkind attention to them. They very quickly took to her. In fact, for some weeks after that visit, my mother liked her a lot more than I did. She thought her company would do me good.

One of the things that annoyed me about Julie was when I found she was booking herself out of school to come and have meals with us – and then going off somewhere else. There was plenty of freedom in that school, but the Principals did get a little old-fashioned about winter evenings. I taxed Julie about it – I felt slighted by her secret wanderings, as if it were *my* company she were trying to avoid. But this was far from the truth, and she came to tea two or three days running after that, just to prove it.

I suppose *harum-scarum* or *tom-boy* are the sort of words that one might be tempted to use to describe her, but they would be wide of the mark. They would suggest a wild sort of kid who hadn't shown much sign yet that one day she was going to settle down into a woman, and that wasn't true of Julie. She was as precocious – and feminine – as any girl at the Powder Mill – only she hadn't much patience with all the immature sex-talk. I sometimes had the feeling (which didn't help me to be more comfortable in her company) that if ever she had been up to anything in railway waiting-rooms, it would have been strictly in the service of science – and something that she would *not* have wanted to talk about.

She told me that she had to be independent or die. But where did she get to on her jaunts? She had several ports of call. She was a girl who talked to absolutely everybody – old men sitting on kitchen-chairs in their doorways, men working in fields, women queuing in the Post Office. They all considered her a bit weird at first, but Julie was never one to let herself be put off by a first show of cold shoulder. She persevered; she wanted to *know* things – and to know people. And people soon discovered, not only that she was harmless, but that she could actually be quite nice – and was a mine of information about the incredible Powder Mill School, always a welcome talking-point in Peak Low. So she was always being asked in for a cup of tea here or a slice of cake there. Perhaps I should also mention that she had a fantastic appetite and was known as a fabulous organiser of feasts from improbable sources.

One of her 'friends', most unexpectedly, was an old man called Tuppy Ibberson, who lived on his own in a filthy hovel at the back of Carrington Brow. He died before the end of the war, and his cottage simply fell down and disappeared of its own accord. He was a nasty, cantankerous old character, and I am still surprised that she managed to wheedle herself past his front door. But it wasn't tea and cakes she got there; it was talk. It was from him that she first heard the story of the runaway couple two hundred years ago. There always has been a legend about the old ruin in Drydale and if you asked people you got different accounts of what was really supposed to have happened there. I don't know quite what version Julie had heard from Tuppy Ibberson – but none of the tales were quite like the one that was printed in a booklet a year or two after the end of the war.

The point is that Julie was fascinated. She told th story in the school dormitory. She even told it to Miss Longhorsley. Wherever she went, she asked people questions about Drydale, comparing versions of the legend, hankering for more facts. People became fed up with it. My mother used to pretend to cover her ears at the very sight of her, and when my father saw her coming along the street, he used to shout, 'It all happened before my time, you know.'

Then Sally Mason came into the village, brought by a lieutenant who looked hardly more than a boy. You can imagine what effect *he* had on the Piers Plowmanites. And we met her one day, two or three days after he'd gone away again, up in the hills when we were out on a *Regional Study*. I was ashamed, the way the girls crowded round her, asking her silly questions, *personal* questions, and generally pulling her leg. They said things like, 'Are you really going to marry him when he comes back? I wouldn't want to get married and have to ask a man's permission every time I wanted to buy a new coat. Whose parents is it who won't let you marry, yours or his?' She looked terribly uncomfortable. She was nice-looking without being beautiful. She was young for her age, which wasn't all that much, anyway. I'd describe her as simple in the very nicest sense of the word. And she was easy meat for Piers Plowman.

You must not look to me for evidence about what happened next. I do not know where you could possibly go now for the facts. All I can tell you is worse than hearsay – it is part hearsay and part guess-work. The surprising thing is that it was Miss Longhorsley who was responsible for the clampdown on real information. I have presented a very imperfect picture of her, because she could be an absolute terror when she wanted to. She even succeeded in pulling the wool over the eyes of the police, when the reputation of her school was at stake. Half the time she seemed lax, dreamy, you'd have thought she belonged to some different world, didn't know what was going on all around her. Then suddenly, something would happen, and she would bestir herself. She could put a hypnotic effect on that school, on the rare occasions when she ever felt moved to. They were a stupid, impressionable set of kids, and she could put a sense of guilt over them that could silence the Powder Mill. In any case, they'd plenty to feel guilty about, some of them, in the weeks after the murder. You'd hardly believe that we could have been stopped from discussing that; but we were. No one would have dared to bring the subject up.

As far as I have ever been able to put things together, it was a group of three or four girls who decided to play a prank on Sally Mason. Julie was not one of them; she was dead against the idea from the start. There was talk of a sheet of notepaper with the royal coat of arms on it, which might pinpoint it to a girl called Doris Hislop. Her father was in the Civil Service, and she was always flaunting official stationery about the school. But it might not have been her; anybody could get a sheet of paper off her, at a price.

These girls coaxed it out of Sally Mason what day the lieutenant was supposed to return, and they sent a wicked message up to her at Mrs Bramwell's where she was lodging. It wasn't supposed to be *from* the lieutenant – that would have involved them in handwriting difficulties. But it was about him. I can't give the exact words, but roughly it said that owing to the military situation his leave had been stopped, and his unit were standing by to go to France. He wasn't going to be put off, however, by mere fear of a court martial. He was going to break bounds, and would meet her in Drydale at dawn, the day before he was expected. I never saw the letter. I am offering no guarantee that I have got its contents even approximately correct. But I know those girls well enough to be sure that whatever the actual wording, it would be pretty devilish.

Down in Drydale, they were going to give the poor girl a terrible scare. The details again, I am afraid, are even more vague. Julie knew more about them than she was ever prepared to say. She refused to discuss the matter, even with me. I know that somehow or other they were going to stage-manage a repetition of the events of 1758.

Just what they planned, just what actually happened, I don't know. Miss Longhorsley gated the school while the police enquiries were on. We were all questioned – in Miss Longhorsley's presence – and the three or four Herne Hillers who'd been most closely involved were too dead scared to say a word. Even my parents, who were as law-abiding a couple as ever you'd hope to meet, wouldn't hear of my coming forward to suggest that there were people who knew more than they admitted. It was better to stay out of such things. The girls hadn't had anything to do with the actual killing, had they? That was obvious. Why then stir up trouble that need not be? Peak Low is good at keeping itself to itself.

I suppose it was obvious – that the girls had had nothing to do with the murder, I mean. Sometimes I woke up sweating in the night, and wondered if perhaps they had carried their play-acting too far, and something had got out of hand, and there had been a terrible accident. But I could not picture in what circumstances. The police were concentrating on a soldier's knife, almost brand new, that had been found near the scene of the murder, and it was almost a consolation to believe that the crime was something to do with the Anti-Aircraft troops along the Peak Forest road.

And what did Julie Patterson know about it all? For some reason or other she was kept in the sanatorium while the police were on the premises. I couldn't help thinking at the time that this was a Longhorsley device – but I must admit that she looked pretty washed up when eventually she did reappear.

In my own mind I was able to exonerate her. She loathed the set who went in for that kind of thing; and there was a whisper that she had been at the centre of a fiendish dormitory row the previous night. I do know that Julie was up and about very early on the fatal morning. She went out on the pretext of wanting to paint the sunrise; that was the sort of inspiration for which Miss Longhorsley could be a sucker.

My belief has always been that Julie went out to warn the Mason girl. I believe that she was too late, and that she found her already dead. But whether Julie actually witnessed the murder, I have never known.

I will try to answer any questions, but what I have written is the whole truth as far as I know it.

CHAPTER NINE

'Well, Shiner?'

'There's a lot of supposition about it, but I fancy that mostly Mrs Broomhead supposes right. Those girls can be bitches at fifteen and sixteen.'

'They can be bitches at five, Shiner. Now I want you to take a little night walk. There's one question I can't wait to ask Annie Broomhead, and I have to stay here. A man's coming to identify Julie Wimpole. Telex from County. That's the moment I've been waiting for.'

I hesitated a second or two.

'And the question?'

'Oh, yes. Had Julie a stammer when they were kids at the Powder Mill? Because if she had – '

The room in which we had talked to Mrs Broomhead this morning was now a beehive of family activity. She-herself was ironing with an oblique view of the tele-vision; her husband, a small balding man with his collar and tie over the arm of his chair, was watching a celebrity panel game; a girl was doing homework on a corner of the dining-table: an exercise in Venn dia-grams; a younger boy was gluing the struts of a balsa-wood aircraft. The woman was worried to see me. The man turned down the sound of the set. They made to send the children upstairs, but I told them there was no need. I asked my single question.

'Oh, but of course. She always did have that halt in her speech – a sort of constriction. She never let it stand in her way, though. She talked about four times as much as any normal girl. Somehow it seemed to rivet people's attention. It seemed to make you sympathise with what she was saying. Is that all?'

She looked at me in some surprise.

'That's all – unless you've thought of anything you'd like to add to your statement?'

'No, there's nothing, Mr Wright. You do know, don't you, that all this has me out of my depth?'

'The depth wasn't of your digging, Mrs Broomhead.'

'Bad business,' Broomhead said, a corner of his eye still on the silenced screen.

'It *is* a bad business. Were you in Peak Low in Dunkirk year?'

'No. I was in Dunkirk. But I'm a foreigner, anyway. I'm from Barber Booth, all of four miles away. Peak Low doesn't let me into its secrets.'

I called at the constable's house on my way back. Kenworthy had assigned me several chores, and I wanted to get them under way. We could hardly expect definitive answers tonight, but stuff ought to start dribbling back to us early tomorrow. It was worth having P.C. Harrison in the room while I phoned, to see his incredulity when I asked Scotland Yard to ring us back with the lines of a speech from *Hamlet*: the most efficient drill was to canalise all our queries through one desk. Then there were the two other quotations:

Nurse, oh my love is slain and *There are a thousand paths to the delectable tavern of death –*

I made the night-duty clerk read them back to me, enjoying his disbelief. I was learning fast from Kenworthy.

'What am I supposed to do with this lot, Sergeant?'

'Get them to somebody who knows about poetry.'

'And ask him what?'

'Where they come from. What they mean to him. What they meant in their original setting. And whether he has any views as to why a murdered woman should jot them down just before it all started happening.'

'Tonight?'

'Soonest.'

'Bloody roll on!'

'It's for Kenworthy.'

'Yes, Sergeant. Tonight.'

'And there's one more job, but it will have to wait till morning, but get on to it as soon as people's offices start opening. There's a firm of printers – '

I went back to the Three Horseshoes, and again Kenworthy was in conference in the otherwise empty lounge. This time his subject was a middle-aged man in a sober blue suit, with a quiet but not too new art silk tie. He had a Civil Servant's black brief-case on a chair beside him. And this time Kenworthy did interrupt himself to put me in the picture.

'Meet Mr George Dugdale. Mr Dugdale reads his daily paper, and at once recognised the portrait of Julie Wimpole, which is a great tribute to an artist who had to work in limiting circumstances. Mr Dugdale has had to be in court all day, with which you and I can readily sympathise, so he has had to put off coming to help us until now. And he has already stopped off at the mortuary and signed an affidavit of identification. Which is why, if the expense account won't run to the double whisky that you see before him, I shall pay for it out of my own pocket.'

Kenworthy could sound sincere when he wanted to. I duly registered Kindness-to-Dugdale night. And Dugdale looked over at me, raking in all the sympathy he could, conscious that he had undergone a harrowing experience, a culmination of harrowing experiences that had started with the virgin folded newspaper beside his breakfast plate.

'Mr Dugdale is a busy man, Sergeant Wright. He is Senior Probation Officer for the Lancashire Division of Halliton-cum-Stansby. *Mrs* Wimpole was also a Probation Officer, one of his team. She has been currently taking her annual leave. They had a picture postcard from her in the office. And like the postcards received by other individuals on their staff – Bill, Cath, B & S, and T – all those, in fact, whose names were bracketed together in the note-book, it appeared to have been posted in Salford. Sent from here under cover to an accommodation address, I've no doubt. Mrs Wimpole appears to have been very keen indeed not to let people know where she was.'

'Yet equally keen,' I suggested, 'to give signs of continued existence.'

'Neat point, Sergeant Wright. And now, Mr Dugdale, if you can bear with a deluge of questions – and Sergeant, please do interrupt – '

Kindness-to-Sergeants night, too.

'Now, Mr Dugdale. How long had Mrs Wimpole been working with you?'

'Coming up to nine years. She came to us in 1948, a post-war trainee.'

'So now there's a hole in your work-strength,' Kenworthy explored.

'Look, Inspector, I know that you people don't always see eye to eye – '

'I see eye to eye with anyone who's toiling in the same vineyard, Mr Dugdale.'

'Well, I'll be honest with you about Julie, Mr Kenworthy. She got through a mountain of work – but she was a strange mixture. Like anyone else who's of any earthly use in this post-war world, she knew how to make herself a bloody nuisance. Of all the people I've ever had on my staff, the only ones who really pulled their weight were those who weren't afraid to be a pain in the neck on occasion.'

'I've had sergeants like that.'

'She'd an independent streak in her. Sometimes she rocked the boat. I'll admit, I've had to carpet her in my time; usually for keeping information to herself that ought to have been shared.'

'What sort of information?'

'Run-of-the-mill stuff. Trivial really, often enough. Background colour about youngsters in her care. I remember one case where she decided on her own initiative that a rogue deserved another chance that the magistrates weren't likely to give him, and she pulled a fast one on the Bench. In the outcome, I only saved her bacon by covering up for her myself. What it amounted to was that she herself had provided the young sod with an alibi. No one believed it, but we couldn't disprove it, either. That was pure Julie. What she believed in, she did. And sometimes she'd no sense at all about departing from the book, or of thinking ahead about how you were going to get out of it, if you did trip up. She'd her own moral code: and I'm not saying it was a bad one. But it wasn't always Home Office.'

I could easily picture Dugdale becoming a pain in the neck, too – but not to his superiors.

'Was she a Christian?' Kenworthy asked.

'In what sense?'

'I'm wondering how much it might have mattered to her to have a church wedding.'

'May I come back to that in a little while? I'm sure it would be better to – '

'Take your own time, Mr Dugdale.'

'She could be suggestible, too. She made mistakes – which of us doesn't? Sometimes she allowed herself to be conned: an occupational hazard, but there is such a thing as taking care. I'm not saying that she made a saint out of every villain, but she did out of some. The trouble with Julie was she always went the whole hog. When she did drop a clanger, it clanged. May I give you an example? We'd a young hellion called Norris: pilfering, borrowing cars, back-alley protection racket amongst his own kind. We gave him all the chances. But there's such a thing as incompatibility of tempera-ment, even in our line of business, and Norris and the colleague he was assigned to just didn't get on. I was daft enough to transfer him to Julie's list at her request. From then on, she was full of Norris. She was going to show us. She played on his musical talents, got him in with some lads who were forming an amateur band. Stood guarantee for him to hire-purchase a tenor saxophone – which he flogged for twenty quid after the first down-payment. Julie was stuck as his sponsor – and it took your people three weeks to find him. And it wasn't enough for Julie just to admit she'd been taken. She went in for torments of blaming herself – convinced herself that in some way she'd failed *him*. An idealist – some of the time – not fighting the real things, running a private war against things she projected out of herself.'

Dugdale blew out his cheeks, almost breathless with the emphasis he had been putting over. I thought that the death of Julie Wimpole had hit him harder than he had so far admitted.

'The way I'm talking, you must be thinking she was pure liability. I mustn't paint too black a picture, but I'm trying to show all sides of her, and perhaps it's as well to get the unhappy things over first. At her best she was brilliant – and she was often at her best. Some-times she succeeded with cases that would have flum-moxed anyone else in the division, myself included, I don't mind admitting. Sometimes she really did catch a kid's fancy – a boy's or a girl's – some hard-boiled yobbo with a trail of breaking and entering that led back to his Sunday School days; or some fifteen-year-old tart who already knew her way round the park railings. When Julie did click, then things started happening. She could create a personal loyalty in the most unexpected places. When people started leaning over to please her, they seldom back-tracked. I can point to one youth, now a sergeant in the Royal Marines, who'd already got his toes round the Borstal door when I chucked his file over to Julie.'

I thought it was time that I reminded Kenworthy that I was listening.

'Tell me, Mr Dugdale: this is highly exacting and personal work. Didn't her stammer affect her performance?'

'Probably her greatest asset, Sergeant. And don't get me wrong; I've known kids poke fun at her; but never after the first visit. When they started taking the mickey, she just stopped talking, half shutting her eyes in a hooded way that she had, and then starting up again, when they'd worked it out of themselves – stammering worse than ever, on purpose. Basically she couldn't help it; but she knew what it was worth to her. I remember once, she was being cross-examined on oath by a prosecuting solicitor – and she would have stopped short of perjury. But there were one or two things about the case that it was better for the lad's sake not to have revealed. And she wore that lawyer's patience down in the most natural way possible. He dismissed her with half his key questions unasked. She was cunning: but only in the service of what she thought right.'

Kenworthy came in again.

'Presumably, somewhere along the line, there was a Mr Wimpole?'

'Indeed there was. She was married very young, very early, very soon after leaving school, the wildness of the war. It wasn't something that she cared to talk about, and she put out an aura that stopped people fishing. She'd been on my strength a year or more before she mentioned it to me – and then strictly of her own accord. For some reason she suddenly wanted to talk, and I let her. The man was in the Air Force. They met at a station dance that she went to with a friend. It was immediate, idyllic, passionate, blinded them both to all else about them. They thought they might as well be banking a marriage allowance. She said if you counted up the nights that they actually spent together, it came in all to twenty-three.'

'And he came home on a prayer without the wing?' Kenworthy asked.

'No. No wings. A propeller on his arm. He was a Leading Aircraftman: armament fitter. He was cycling round the perimeter track at dusk, when a Wellington coming in to land took his head off with its undercarriage.'

A suitable second for silence. The landlord came in and made up the fire. We hadn't asked for the private use of this room, but it seemed to have become ours. And people already knew where to find us. At this moment, P.C. Harrison knocked and came in with a document. It was addressed to me, and I opened it at once. It had been taken down by phone in Harrison's level-best handwriting on Constabulary notepaper.

To be or not to be, that is the question.

Whether 'tis nobler in the mind to suffer –

I did not read it all through there and then. I laid the paper down where it could catch Kenworthy's eye if he wanted it to. He didn't.

'They say that the other things will take a bit longer,'

the policeman said. 'Probably won't be through till morning.'

'I'm not surprised.'

Harrison cast a curious eye over the three of us, and at Dugdale's glass of Scotch. Kenworthy and I weren't drinking.

'Good night, Constable.'

'Had she ever said anything to you about Peak Low?' Kenworthy asked.

'Had she! Believe me, she was a menace. It was her favourite story – one of our standing jokes in the office. It didn't take much to get Julie on to Peak Low.'

'Which part of the story?'

'How many parts has it? There was something that happened here centuries ago; a young woman eloping had been killed. And then there was a mirror-crime in the early war years. Julie's school had been evacuated here.'

'We have managed to detect that. Did she tell you that she had actually met that young woman?'

'No.'

Dugdale seemed surprised.

'Or that there was some connection or other between her school and the killing?'

'She never said anything like that.'

'Then what did she say?'

'She told us about the unusual way in which people can get married here. Something about a Judge Peculiar and a Spiritual Court. For some reason it fascinated her.'

'For what reason?'

'Because it was unconventional, I suppose. Because it was rooted in a romantic past. Because it had provided a way in which some couples at least had managed to defeat their environment.'

'And if she were thinking of marrying again, you think she'd have liked to be married here in Peak Low?'

'Inspector Kenworthy, how can I answer a question like that? It's only my impression you want, isn't it? Well, then, I'll say yes. But if you ask me my reasons, you'll find them unsatisfactory.'

'You mean, you're only going by her temperament?'

'Her disposition. She seemed to think that Peak Low was something special to her. It was a feeling that had grown over the years.'

'To your knowledge, did she ever come back here before now?'

'To my knowledge, never. She often talked of doing so, but she never got round to it. That was another office joke.'

'But you do think she'd have preferred a church wedding to a Register Office?'

'I have no reason for saying so, but I'll stick my neck out and say yes. You asked me earlier if I considered her a Christian, and really I have no right to answer that. But I think she was. Or, put it this way, she was an intensely religious woman in a non-church-going way. She didn't belong to anything or anybody. She was totally freelance. I've heard her say that if you do have a spiritual belief, then logically it must be the biggest thing in your life. She had a spiritual belief. I wouldn't venture to enlarge on its complexities.'

Kenworthy pulled the *Hamlet* extract towards him with the tips of his fingers, glanced down at it, then slid it away again.

'So now, Mr Dugdale, we come to the critical question: have you any reason to suppose that Mrs Wimpole was contemplating marriage?'

'Yes.'

There was a new gravity in the monosyllable. I thought I even detected a crack in Dugdale's voice.

'I'm afraid so. Do you mind if I buy myself another whisky?'

'Do.'

Kenworthy did not offer to pay for this one.

'And "afraid so" is about as far as I would like to go. I'm a totally useless witness, aren't I? I can't give chapter and verse to any of my thunderbolts.'

'Is it such a thunderbolt, Mr Dugdale?'

'To me it is. In a moment, I hope you'll see why. It happened one evening in March this year. We had a man on our books who should never have been there. He was not a suitable subject for probation, and I had said so roundly and unequivocally in my report to the Bench – so uncompromisingly that I think they resented it, thought I was trying to pre-empt them. James Harbutt: and a string of aliases to which I've no doubt your Record Office could add. He had a long list of convictions, usually for confidence tricks of a mean rather than an ambitious nature: credit by means of a trick, and charges of that sort. The latest one, for which he was up before the Halliton court, was for obtaining refreshment and lodging at an inn without either the means or intention of paying for it. But to see the way he was dressed, and the sort of suitcase he was carrying, you could hardly blame the receptionist. And God knows why the Bench should have taken it in their heads that morning to take pity on him. Sometimes these lay justices just feel they have to assert their lunatic independence. Harbutt's solicitor – free legal aid, of course – spun a yarn about his having gone straight for eighteen months. They made a probation order: and Harbutt listened like a model penitent while the clerk explained the terms of it.'

Dugdale took a sip from his glass.

'The first time he failed to keep an appointment, I wasn't surprised. I'd taken his file myself, and waited an hour one evening for him. Then I went home, Julie was working late, typing case-notes, and Harbutt came in panting, shot a line about how he'd been held up and was worried stiff about letting me down. She told him she was sure it would be all right, she'd let me know he'd been in with the best of intentions, and he'd better be in to see me himself as soon as he could. They seemed to have stayed talking for hours – until the care-taker started prowling querulously on the stairs. And the next morning, Julie came to me and asked me if Harbutt's file could be transferred to her list. I refused outright. Harbutt was the wrong sort of case for her; she'd fall for his promises right, left and centre. Cutting out detail, it reached me along the grapevine a month or so later that Julie had taken to meeting this man. There are one or two pubs on the moors on the Lanca-shire–Yorkshire border that are ideal for that sort of assignation – though they are seldom as secure as the blindfolded couples seem to think. I took her on one side about it – and got what I ought to have expected. She was a free agent; neither the Home Office nor the Court of Common Pleas had any jurisdiction over her private life. And if I was going to cull any plums out of *Becoming Conduct for Servants of the Crown*, this was 1957 and we had fought a war for, amongst other things, the right of the individual to free association.'

'She didn't deny the liaison?'

'Not for a minute.'

'And how far did they go?'

'Mr Kenworthy – what can I say to that? Julie was not made of wood. Harbutt had a history with women; he'd slept with some of his most lucrative dupes. If

Harbutt was getting satisfaction out of Julie, it wasn't park-railing stuff. He was an advanced performer, a connoisseur – you might say, a qualified demonstrator. And you could see the difference in Julie. She'd been drifting into mousiness. She suddenly went shopping, had altogether more bounce about her, more flash in her eyes.'

'And Harbutt was staying out of trouble?'

'I used the phrase just now: he became a model penitent.'

So what were you worried about?

Kenworthy didn't put the question, so I knew I mustn't.

'And there's another thing, Mr Kenworthy. Right from the start I've associated Harbutt with Peak Low. The caretaker, that first night, heard them talking about the place. Even for Julie, that seemed odd.'

'And what has been Harbutt's reaction to Julie's death?'

'How can I know that? I only saw her picture in the paper this morning. And I've been in court all day.'

Kenworthy let him go shortly after that. He faced a wearisome drive home over a spur on the Pennines. Now Kenworthy looked out the Wimpole edition of *Hamlet*, and we looked at the two versions together.

'The idea of *the sea* is still in. It was Julie who decided to call it *troubled*. Shakespeare *takes arms*; Julie *enlaces* them. *Heart-ache* comes up twice, but *communion*'s new. *A consummation devoutly to be wished* is common to Peak Low and Stratford-on-Avon. That's waiting for marriage, if anything ever was. And I was right about *Perchance to dream*. The *nightmare*'s all Julie's.'

He got up and scraped his pipe-bowl into the fire-place.

'I don't think we went far wrong earlier on, Shiner.

She was pretending to be Hamlet, seeing, in fact, what there might be in those lines for her. Indecision, misery – and the promise of a consummation that might turn into nightmare. How did you make out with Mrs Broomhead?'

'Julie had always had the stammer.'

'I thought as much. So there are quite a lot of people who have been concealing from us the fact that they recognised her: Will Beard on the bus, Cantrell as she stood looking round with the suitcase, the men in the public bar. Peter Lovelock.'

'Who's Peter Lovelock?'

'Cantrell's friend, the one we think Julie wanted to avoid. And Julie had talked to all and sundry. A lot of people must have known for certain where they'd heard that vocal delivery before – especially in conjunction with an interest in Drydale. Shiner – there's conspiracy here – intuitive herd conspiracy. And it's fear that's behind it – not fear of us, fear of something they all know; fear of letting each other down.'

We walked across the street to our lodgings; a drear November night with a mist shading haloes round the lighted cottage windows. Kenworthy wished me good night, and said he was going over to the police-house to make some calls on his own account. No; he'd attend to them himself. But somehow I had the impression for the first time in that clammy rising vapour that he now looked upon me as if I was on the case with him.

CHAPTER TEN

Obviously we had to go to Halliton the next morning, and Kenworthy was impatient for an early start. And I was equally eager, almost, I suppose, to the point of being on edge, to see whether anything had come in from my overnight enquiries. It seemed unlikely that anything effective could yet have been achieved; yet here it was – Time of Origin 0402 hours. What greybeard had the Yard yanked out of his slumbers to look at a tag of poetry? Perhaps scholars keep odd hours, or sleep hardly at all; perhaps a tag of poetry, albeit sleep-destroying, can be a joy to some.

Nurse, o my love is slaine, I saw him goe
O'r the white Alpes alone.

It will be noticed that this commentator prefers the seventeenth-century orthography. The lines are from John Donne's Elegie XVI – To his Mistris.

There followed some rather snide stuff about the interpretation of the imagery on parallel planes, and the probable response of the superficial reader. There was a lot of high-minded analysis that was well over my head. But I read it all.

These lines are generally considered to be frankly sexual, a fact perhaps made respectable by the ultimate elevation of their author to the Deanery of St Paul's. The speaker is a young girl temporarily exiled from her lover, and is being advised not to waken her servant-companion in a nightmare memory of her last orgasm. The Alpes over which she views her lover's deflorescence are her own breasts, and the form and nature of his death is plainly phallic, as shewn by the ensuing line:

95

Nurse, o my love is slaine, I saw him goe
O'r the white Alpes alone; I saw him I
Assail'd, fight, taken, stabb'd, bleed, fall and die.

'Dirty-minded old bugger,' Kenworthy said. 'A lot of these academics are. Still I'm always ready to settle for a sexy explanation. It wouldn't be far under Julie's surface, and Harbutt seemed to have been an Academy Award man.'

But even with our literary education thus extended, our departure was further delayed. Kenworthy was driving, and was just letting in the clutch when P.C. Harrison, in shirt-sleeves, came gesticulating to his gate.

'Telephone for Sergeant Wright.'

Kenworthy fumed. When I returned we were in motion before I had fairly closed the passenger door. I must actually have smirked.

'Well?'

'Well, at least we now know the identity of *Mantillus*.'

'Who?'

He did not like efforts at dramatic suspense that did not come from himself.

'Julie Wimpole.'

'The stupid bitch,' he said, wholly unjustly.

For all his impatience, he drove with a certain text-book attention to detail that would have done a test-examiner proud. We swept over a fringe of peat moor, then settled into a valley bottom with a murky little river and the tiered windows of Victorian cotton-mills dominating nodal villages. Somewhere south of Stockport he pulled unexpectedly into a lay-by under a high and grimy wall.

'A long time ago, Shiner, but probably only yesterday sometime, I implied that I was interested in the manner in which three young ladies were enticed from

96

their lodgings at dawn to take an unlikely walk to an uninviting ruin. And in one case we were given a plausible answer: the girls at the Powder Mill sent Sally Mason a diabolically composed letter on crown notepaper.'

'That had the ring of truth about it, in my ears.'

'And mine, Shiner. But let's jump a step. Do we forgive the immediate investigating officers for not getting on to the Powder Mill angle?'

'I think so,' I said. 'Thanks to Miss Longhorsley's guile. The girls scared out of their wits, too petrified to talk. 1940: police short-handed, and plenty of other things on people's minds. Plus the fact that for a certainty they thought that a lost pen-knife at an army camp was much nearer the mark. I presume they had a good look for footprints? Various people swanning about in the early morning – '

'There were people swanning about day in, day out, Shiner – especially with the school in residence. And you don't leave tell-tale marks in dry grass in a limestone valley in May. What's worrying me more is what happened to that letter. Why was it never found? If she'd left it behind in her lodgings, and I can't think of anything less likely, it would surely have been turned in by her landlady. If she'd had it with her in Drydale, it would have been found in her handbag. She hadn't been robbed and her petty belongings hadn't been disturbed. Therefore – '

'Therefore it was retrieved by whoever had delivered it.'

'Sound sense – and what sort of chap was he?'

'Someone who was playing along with the girls?'

'Yes: I think it had to be a man, because the aim was to scare Sally Mason, and I doubt whether the girls alone could have done that. Now what sort of boyfriends would girls like that have gone for?'

'Any they could get,' I said. 'Someone about their own age.'

'No. Any they could get, yes. But not about their own age. Adolescent girls, out for real kicks, go for someone a little bit older, Shiner. Less callow, a bit nearer real business. All surmise this – but it's giving me a sense of direction. A village hoyboy, out to play a prank, would be willing to do his stuff. He'd also have the common sense to want to get that letter back – yes?'

'Makes sense.'

'But would he go poking about for it round a body that was in quite such a mess as Sally Mason would be? We know what Julie Wimpole looked like. Wouldn't he turn tail?'

'In nine cases out of ten, probably. But how can we be sure?'

'Never mind about being sure. Just let's explore probability. I say he'd run for it. Therefore –'

'Therefore the letter's still in existence somewhere.'

'That's not what I mean. The letter wasn't there. Therefore it had been taken. Leaving us with an ugly *probability* – something that to my old-fashioned mind seems unclean. That the killing was done by the same man who had an interest in getting his hands on the letter.'

'The village hoyboy.'

'Nasty,' Kenworthy said. 'Unaesthetic. Killing for killing's sake. Blood-lust. I can't say I want things to end up that way, but it's something to bear in mind when we get back tonight.'

He reached for the ignition switch. Soon we were in an extended conurbation: traffic lights every thirty or forty yards, bus-stops, parked vehicles – and, it seemed, a secret local Highway Code when it came to filtering at junctions. Do-It-Yourself Stores, Pet Food Shops, and littered newsagents' forecourts. Halliton (cum-Stansby) was a blur of town-centre, only separated from other town-centres by overlapping town outskirts: a parish church of blackened stone, a bus-station, a market-place, a spinning mill with Gothic turrets under weathered copper roofs.

We were expected in the Probation Office: two flights of lino-covered stairs through a side entrance. Somewhat alarmingly we passed the kitchen fire-exit of a Chinese restaurant that functioned round the other corner of the street. Dugdale had put his office at our disposal. It measured some eight feet by seven, a sort of inner cupboard within a suite of cupboards. A stack of over-spilling manilla folders had been laid on the desk for us, and on the blotter a summary of Julie Wimpole's work-load at the beginning of her leave. Dugdale was hovering.

'Nothing but routine: shoplifting, store-breaking and general larceny. Difficult to know whether anyone might have had it in for her. I'd say not, but you never can be certain. Harbutt's reporting at eleven.'

We looked through the records, but could not infuse much life into them. There was a good deal of Julie Wimpole's work in typed minutes, flimsies of court reports, marginalia in her own hand. All very efficient; objective memoranda in the style that she had favoured in her notebook, a tendency to save split seconds by omitting mere vowels. There was no sarcasm, or even attempted wit to brighten her notes, even her personal ones. It was plain workmanship, obviously thorough – and there was a very great deal of it. She had been a phenomenally hard worker.

'Let's see what you've got on friend Harbutt.'

Dugdale had his file ready: beginning with a transcript of his record. It filled out what we already knew, but gave us nothing that screamed urgently for a fresh approach. As Dugdale had said, Harbutt had operated under several aliases: Crowson in Sheffield in 1946, Challis in Birmingham in '49, Pitts in Liverpool in '52. There had been restful periods when he had been compelled to leave the field at the mercy of his competitors. And his specialities had included door-to-door salesmanship, seducing housewives almost on their thresholds and then weighing in with blackmail demands that were modest enough to succeed. There was an underlying warp of moderation about Harbutt's targets. It might have stemmed from lack of confidence, but was probably carefully calculated prudence; small profits and quick returns.

Kenworthy stood and looked out of the window: yards, the bell-tower of a Victorian primary school, a Congregational chapel, a car-park in a slum-clearance desert: a garishly painted Standard Eight with rust-holes in its wings. Kenworthy called Dugdale over: 'Whose?'

'Young blood. Noisy but harmless. Got the open-air bug, and a touch of religion, *pro tem*. It all helps.'

'On your firm's books?'

'One of them was Julie's, up to a year ago. One of the brighter boys, knew which side his bread was buttered. We got his order discharged six months before it was due to expire. One of her triumphs.'

'We think he may have been in Peak Low on Julie's first Sunday.'

'Very likely. They're out and about most weekends.'

'And Julie was anxious to avoid him. Left her drink practically untouched.'

'That figures,' Dugdale said. 'If Matt Caley spotted her, it could have been all over Halliton by Monday morning.'

'Got his notes handy?'

We went through his file, and his conviction had been for taking an untended car and abandoning it in Blackpool. Julie Wimpole had scribbled in the margin, 'The sooner this lad buys a banger of his own, the sooner he'll respect other people's.'

'I'd like a word with Caley before we leave town,' Kenworthy said.

Then we heard James Harbutt announce himself in the outer office. He was another of these middle to late thirties men, in clean trousers and a brown pullover, clean-shaven, hair trimmed back and sides, but shadows under his eyes and a pallor the shade of newsprint. Events of recent days could have hit him pretty hard, and he must have had at least one bad night.

'Come in and sit down. You have a lot to tell us. Begin where you like.'

'I'll begin by calling myself the biggest fool on this flank of the Pennines.'

'What? For going straight for the last six months?'

'Now, Mr Kenworthy – if you've only come here to take the piss – '

'I'm not taking the piss, comrade. I'm a realist. Get that into your head before you start telling us the tale you've got ready.'

Myself, I wouldn't have approached him in this way; but Kenworthy seemed determined to antagonise him; and that is a recognised ploy.

'All right, Mr Kenworthy. Then I'll be a realist too. I won't even tell you I'm going to go straight from now on. Because I don't even bloody well know whether I shall. For the last six months I could do and I did. I even accepted – and held down – a job on an assembly line. But I don't think I can stomach another shift – not without her behind me.'

It had the ring of conviction. But the ring of conviction had always been Harbutt's stock-in-trade. Sometimes it had led to convictions of a different order.

'I'll let you have it straight, Mr Kenworthy. I'm beginning to wonder if a spell inside now and then isn't a fair price to pay for not standing at a conveyor belt.'

Kenworthy came back surprisingly gently.

'She meant as much to you as that, did she?'

'You didn't know her, did you? You can't have done. She was – a bloody saint, that's what she was.'

The *bloody* was neatly in character. Harbutt's strength was his acting ability, a talent that had extended itself to a habit. He could have written good dialogue, too. He couldn't talk without acting, even when he was playing it straight. It did not make it easy to be sure how straight.

'Do you know what sort of a childhood she had had, Mr Kenworthy? Parents that didn't want either her or each other, and could afford to give her most of the things that she asked for – as if that was any sort of compensation. She grew up to sympathise with the likes of me – and with this lot here.'

He indicated by a sweep of his arm the whole paraphernalia of juvenile delinquency. And I thought too about the reputation of his sexual prowess; was that something that Julie had found a belated need for too?

'Yes,' Kenworthy was saying, taking a tack that I had not expected. 'Oddly enough I can understand her being ready to marry you. But I don't quite see you marrying her.'

'And why the hell not?'

'Don't you think she might have cramped your style?'

'Listen, Kenworthy, maybe I deserve something

more than your opinion of me. I can only assure you – '

'But you didn't marry her, did you? You didn't even set out from Halliton – '

'I'm coming to that.'

'I've no doubt when it comes to the crunch you'll be able to account for all your movements on Thursday, Friday and Saturday. Works card punched at all the right times, pub in reliable company, maybe a soccer match, Saturday afternoon – by which time you ought to have been off on your honeymoon.'

'I said, I was coming to that.'

'Come to it now, boy. Sergeant Wright and I have been known to believe every word a man says – under the right kind of stress.'

Harbutt was under stress now. He did not quite know where to put his hands so we should not see them trembling. I thought there were tears not far behind his voice. But he was a method actor. He knew how to think his way into a part.

'Listen, Kenworthy – and for God's sake *do* listen. All that happened between Julie and me was between our two selves. If you don't hear it from me, you'll not hear it from anyone. Make it easy for me, for Christ's sake.'

'Make it easy for yourself.'

'All right, then. But don't keep interrupting. I'm not stringing you on. I *want* to talk, Kenworthy.'

He made a visible effort to pull himself together. It could have been just that bit too carefully visible.

'It meant everything to Julie, getting married in Peak Low. I expect you've assembled that part of the story. The place was an obsession with her. And speaking for myself, I don't find that too difficult to understand. But there was another big reason why Peak Low suited our book. Here in Halliton was out of the question, because of the hullabaloo. That old sod in there – '

We could hear Dugdale's voice droning in the general office.

'We wanted to be able to come back and just quietly let them know it was all signed, sealed and delivered. There wasn't going to be a honeymoon – only that first weekend. We didn't need a honeymoon, Julie and I. I shall never forget this spring and summer. The likes of it had not come into my life before. But we had to be sure, don't you see? I mean, *I* didn't – I knew; at least, by God, I thought I did. But it was Julie's idea – and I had to give her the escape route she asked for, didn't I? You see, one of us had to spend fifteen nights there. You know all that, don't you? We weren't even going to tell the vicar in advance. Report to him at any reasonable time, that's what the book says. So Julie says, if I'd any second thoughts during that fortnight, I just don't have to turn up. And if she'd any second thoughts, she just wouldn't be there when I did. It was a fortnight's trial parting, to – to see how we'd stand up to it.'

'And you didn't go.'

'By God! – if I'd known what I've known since I picked up yesterday morning's paper! I mean, I could picture what she'd feel like, waiting, and giving up hope, and having to pack up her stuff in the farm-house. But now – '

'What changed your mind for you?' Kenworthy asked. 'And don't tell me you thought you weren't good enough for her.'

'Madness. I felt as if I was getting a sort of kick out of not being there. And then I took to hating *her* for not being *here*. I suddenly thought what a future might be like, being bossed about by her. Oh, God, give me that chance again!'

He buried his face in his hands, and Kenworthy signalled to me to leave him alone for a minute. I thought from the look on Kenworthy's face that he had accepted the gist of what we had just heard; and I must confess that I was relieved to think so. But I was thinking: a long shot had come into my head, as far-fetched and yet as feasible as any that ever came into Kenworthy's. I would have given anything to be able to pull it off here and now. I looked at Kenworthy, begging permission. He nodded. I waited till Harbutt raised his head. His cheeks were tear-stained.

'Harbutt, there was some other connection, wasn't there, between you and Peak Low, something that helped bring you two together, to cement things, as it were?'

He shook his head, looking at me as if he was well aware that I was a very junior partner.

'I must be mistaken, then. I could have sworn it had been mentioned somewhere along the line.'

'I'm a Londoner, Sarge. I'd never heard of the bloody place until I met Julie.'

'No? How many aliases have you ever worked under?'

'What the hell do you want to know that for? Water under the bridge, that.'

'I know. But we do know some of them, you see – Crowson, Challis, Pitts – '

'I'm buggered if I'm having all this dug up again.'

I was nearly there. But the very next answer could make hash of my idea.

'You must have been in the forces at some time or other, a man of your age?'

'I was: the first lot of militia.'

'And what name did you go under then?'

'My own.'

'And which one was that?'

He hesitated. It was the first time throughout this interview that he had paused for thought. I knew he was toying with an outright lie, and it surprises me even yet that he did not tell me one. If he were telling the truth now, there might have been some leading threads of the truth in the rest of what he had told us this morning.

'Challis,' he said.

'Ack-ack?'

'Jesus! Is there no peace?'

I turned to Kenworthy.

'I think we shall find that Gunner Challis was one of those who could not account for his knife at a kit-inspection.'

'One of the six who couldn't,' Harbutt said.

'And what did you tell them you had done with yours?'

'Had it pinched.'

'And what had you actually done with it?'

'Flogged it in the village for seven and six. I could get a new one from the Quarter bloke for four and a tanner.'

'Flogged it to whom?'

'Some bumpkin.'

Kenworthy asked only one question.

'And did Julie know this?'

'Not then. I told her as soon as she mentioned Peak Low.'

Kenworthy was very gracious about it. 'You'll do, Shiner.' It was the most fulsome thing he was to say to me for several years.

Matt Caley was a nineteen-year-old who did not look as if he had ever joy-ridden to Blackpool in his life. He was very anxious to please. Our interview was brisk and short.

'You were in Peak Low a week last Sunday?'

'That's right.'

'And you saw Mrs Wimpole?'

'I was the only one of the gang who did. I just saw her vanishing round the side-door of the pub. I could see she didn't want us to tag on to her, so I kept my mouth shut. Sir, Mrs Wimpole had done a lot for me – '

'We know all about that. You didn't mention to anyone at all that you had seen her?'

'No.'

Then a moment's thought, as if the exception was hardly worth bringing up.

'Well, only to Mr Dugdale. I met him in the Post Office on the Monday morning.'

CHAPTER ELEVEN

Kenworthy asked me to drive us back from Halliton, so it was my turn to apply myself to the Highway Code with the almost pathological finickiness which the public would have the right to demand of a policeman. But Kenworthy was sunk in something deeper than reverie, and he did not speak at all as we edged our way through the peak evening traffic. It was a miserable journey, in a thin drizzle, and we had a worn wiper that squeaked against the screen. Somewhere south of Stockport, the traffic thinned perceptibly. For the first time in twenty miles we emerged from built-up streets, dropped into the last of the industrial valleys and began the long climb beyond it, into a blanket of low-lying cloud. Kenworthy cleaned out his pipe and began to produce a solid blue fog of his own.

At a moorland cross-roads, the visibility was so poor that I had to get out to examine an old-fashioned finger-post. When we moved off again, Kenworthy started talking.

'There's something we've found faintly amusing, Shiner, in the Navajo watch that Peak Low kept on Julie's movements. When she goes for an early-morning walk, there's Bagshaw watching her round the corner of his cow-shed. She stands on a bridge and throws a leaf into a stream; and there's a quarryman looking down from the brow of a hill. She picks up a stone, like the one she's going to be killed with – and a labourer called Rousell is standing stock-still not fifty yards from her.'

'She goes to see Annie Broomhead, and they watch her turn back from the wall overlooking the cottages.'

'Precisely. But what haven't they told us? There's one thing in common, Shiner, in all they've revealed. None of it matters much.'

'Except Annie Broomhead.'

'Perhaps they didn't think we had it in us to work it out as far as Annie's front door. But you can bet *they* had. The girl with the stammer, turning back from the only woman who was at school with her at the Powder Mill? You think they didn't know that? So what else have they kept to themselves?'

We were in the heart of a cloud now on an exposed height. I was having to drive with my nose practically on the windscreen, barely able to pick out the edge of the tarmac.

'So when we get home, Shiner – let's call it that, shall

we, just to complete the misery? – it's a bee-line for the Delectable Tavern. It's follow your nose and it's bluff. We'll go on letting them take us – till it's time for us to take them. The old, old principle. We let them see we know a little, so they think we know more than we do. So then they get careless, and spill us some more. You know the built-in peril?'

'That they'll find our weak spot for themselves.'

'In which case it might lead to no end of fun. I'm not too proud to make an ass of myself in public – are you, Shiner?'

We arrived in the pub car-park at last, and he even had the grace to mumble something about my difficult drive. But the moment the car doors had slammed, he was like a capital ship with its decks cleared for action. He pushed open the door of the lounge bar, as if this were the sort of Commando raid in which one threw in a grenade first, then looked round to see if the place were occupied. As seemed so often the case when we weren't there ourselves, Cantrell and his friend Lovelock were the only ones there. Kenworthy seemed determined to treat them as hostile witnesses: *insolence* is the only word I can find for the way he spoke to them. And they looked, both of them, for an awkward second as if this time they were going to resent it. I kept a poker face. And Kenworthy's appearance of pent-up fury won the day. I believe, looking back, that he had been holding his breath to make the veins stand out at his temples.

'I think we'll have you two beauties across the passage, in the other room.'

They shambled self-consciously in front of us, carrying their pots with them into the public bar. In there, by this hour of the evening, was gathered a useful collection of men: Rousell, the man who had trailed

Julie on her first morning; Will Beard, who had sat next to her on the bus, and who had been connected in the past with some common sexual assault case that had never come to court; two or three quarry-workers who had testified about Julie's movements, including the Sunday lunch-time and the psychedelic car. Kenworthy at once put on a completely different act. He could have fooled me, so I have no doubt he fooled them. He was suddenly casual and benign, bought himself a pint of mild and bitter – I have discovered since that he disliked the mixture so much that he bought it to curb his own drinking.

'Ah! The Shadow Cabinet! Come to any conclusions yet, have we?'

Someone had the nerve to ask him whether *he* had any progress to report. He took this in well-played good part.

'Not quite. Not quite ready to pounce yet. As somebody present may be highly relieved to hear.'

Did anyone's eyes seek momentarily someone else's face? Was anyone anxious to show that he was not looking for some other man's reaction? Did anyone move an eyelid to take in Cantrell and Lovelock? All eyes, in fact, seemed unusually intrigued by the sight of their own tankards.

'We shall need the help of you gentlemen,' Kenworthy said.

Cantrell interrupted to order two more drinks. A gesture of detachment?

'For example, gentlemen, which of you can describe the events in Drydale on that fateful morning?'

Silence; no one was prepared to take the lead on such a blunt one as that. So Bill Hepplewhite, behind the bar, felt obliged to say something. He valued the co-operative reputation of his house.

'Like we've told you before, Mr Kenworthy – she came in here, and she talked about everything under the sun. But apart from that – '

'I wasn't thinking about recent events. I was thinking about the old case.'

'Ah, well, you see, we didn't really know that other girl, what was her name, Mason, except by sight. She was a nice-looking girl, right enough, but on the shy side.'

'I don't mean her, either. I mean the original case.'

Silence.

'Come along, now. Isn't there anyone who can tell me the original story? I can't think you're all tongue-tied when the tourists ask you – with a pint at the end of it.'

'You mean, you just want someone to spin that old yarn again?'

Some old chap then stirred, a bit stiff and stilted at first, in that unnatural atmosphere.

'This girl, you see, she was brought here a couple of hundred years ago by this bloke. And he lodged her up in the hills with some old biddy, and then went away again while she got her residential qualification, as you might say, then some of the lads thought she looked good for a bit of a lark – '

'Some of the lads from this pub, that would be?'

The storyteller did not like the interruption.

'Well, yes, I suppose that would be the case. And they said they found the girl already dead, but the case that was put up was that they'd been in league with the old biddy to rob her and share out. So they all got topped. Then years later the bridegroom-to-be told the truth as he was dying. Someone in the navy. I've no head for history. He's supposed to have come back to get rid of her.'

'But that isn't the story as it used to be told, is it?' Kenworthy asked.

The question puzzled them. It was something they'd never thought about.

'That's how it puts it in the book,' the man Rousell said.

'No. That's not how it puts it in the book. That's how it *suggests* it in the book. That's how it *might* have been. Bad history, that – I have it on the very best authority. But what I'm trying to get at is how the story was told *before* the book was written.'

This floored them. It was a long way back, a long way for memories not attuned to literary analysis. And they were further confounded by wondering what Kenworthy was driving at.

'You wouldn't expect us to know that, Mr Kenworthy.'

'I don't see why not. I just hoped that there might be someone here who'd remember the tale as old Tuppy Ibberson used to tell it.'

This was a body blow. There was not one amongst them with the immediate wit to know that it must be from Annie Broomhead that we had heard of Tuppy Ibberson. Tuppy himself was local lore, of a distant and almost forgotten vintage. It was probably years since his name had been mentioned in here. Kenworthy had achieved his first purpose: he had impressed them.

A moment's rumination, and something came back to them. Someone said, 'Well, the way Tuppy always told it, it was always the village lads who had done it. There were some rough old buggers living round these parts in those days. And there was a song about it, printed on sheets and sold for a penny. And according to that, they'd confessed.'

'Exactly,' Kenworthy said, and seemed delighted at

the statement. They could not see why, and this bewildered them. But he did not give anyone a chance to put in the crucial question. He kept the initiative.

'And if you ask me, there were some rough old buggers in these parts in 1940, too,' he said. 'And some rough young buggers.'

He was looking now for some reason specifically at Will Beard, who did not like this attention.

'Don't look at Will,' someone said helpfully. 'He was away. Pioneer Corps.'

'Not that week, I wasn't,' Beard said suddenly. 'I was home on leave.'

An unexpected moment of gratuitous honesty. For some reason or other, Kenworthy was anxious to smooth over Beard.

'Don't worry, Will. I'm not thinking you did it. The point is, gentlemen, that a certain pattern is beginning to emerge. There were a Rousell and a Hepplewhite amongst the names of those hanged in the eighteenth century. According to the broadsheet, anyway.'

Were there? I couldn't remember. I checked afterwards, and it was a Kenworthy fiction. They were ready to believe anything he told them. He also knew all the right moments at which to needle them.

'And what do you hope to prove from that?' Hepplewhite said.

'Nothing.'

'Then why bring it up?'

'Because of what I'm going to say next. There were also some girls in the village in 1940.'

He looked hopefully round for reactions. In all ordinary circumstances there'd have been exaggerated memories. But surely he didn't hope for titters and sniggers to break up this tension? The screws were too far down for that. And they were disturbed by all his talking round corners. That was why he was doing it.

'There must have been one or two interesting pieces of homework amongst them.'

'They weren't interested in us,' someone said.

'No. But they might have been interested in *you*.'

Kenworthy swung round on Cantrell and Lovelock, then apparently felt in the mood for gratuitous insult.

'Not *you*, Cantrell. You'd be too young for them – though I dare say you chanced your arm. But you, Lovelock – '

'We didn't stand an earthly,' Lovelock said. 'Not with that lot. They hung about the army camp all the time.'

'And if you ask me – ,' Cantrell said.

'Which I don't.'

'If you ask me, instead of talking about Hepplewhites and Rousells, you'd do better to try to call up the army again. There was a knife found down in the valley.'

'I know. It's a pity about that knife. It messed up the issue in 1940, but I'll take good care it doesn't mess me up now. There were six soldiers who couldn't find their knives. So a couple of hundred squaddies in the battery probably never had their movements properly looked at.'

'Then that would let the lads of the village out. I just don't see – '

'I don't expect you to see anything, Cantrell. I've told you before: you were too young. Though you might agree with me that it needn't have been a squaddy who'd lost the knife.'

'It was a soldier's knife.'

'Of the sort that any Boy Scout would have given his ears for? Were you ever a Scout, Cantrell? Were you, Lovelock?'

They couldn't deny that, and somehow there wasn't

time for them to deny possession of soldiers' knives, either: not that that would have carried weight as evidence. In a split second, Kenworthy was appealing to the generous reasonableness of the whole company, smiling round them all with benevolence and logic.

'So let's not beat about the bush. Nobody's going to get done at this range for receiving four and a tanner's worth of best Sheffield cutlery. There was a traffic in knives. Does anyone want to deny that?'

Crafty: no one dared.

'So which of you had one?'

Apparently no one.

'Did *you*?'

He picked on one poor old devil with teeth like a *cheval de frise*.

'I do seem to remember – '

Hepplewhite came again to the rescue. He had to be master of ceremonies in his own pub.

'Well, look at it this way, Mr Kenworthy. Sometimes these Gunners came in here on Wednesdays and Thursdays without the price of a pint. Obviously we daren't run up a slate.'

'I can see that.'

'There was one man particularly – '

Harbutt – alias Challis – alias –?

' – who seemed to have an endless supply of knives. If you ask me, he'd nicked them from the Q Stores.'

'Very probably. I'm not thinking of charging him with it, but *you* had one – '

This was aimed at Lovelock.

'If I say No, you can't prove that I did.'

'And you lost it.'

'And I'm bloody sure you couldn't prove that, either. In fact, I didn't. I dare say I could still find it at home somewhere, amongst my old junk.'

'Which wouldn't prove anything, either.'

This seemed to satisfy Kenworthy for the time being about the knives. We had another of his rapid changes of subject and tone. Now we came back to the girls.

'Toffee-nosed crew, then, were they?'

No willingness to agree. He had to jolly them patiently along. There were men here who had nothing particular to hide, but had learned in the last ten minutes that it was better not to tangle with Kenworthy. Counter-productive is the word they use for it, in the economic sciences.

'There must be someone here who got his fingers burned, surely? What's the matter with you all? Are you all scared that I'm preparing a secret statement at the request of your wives?'

This might at any other time have been good for a light laugh, but not now. Unexpectedly it was Will Beard who loosened the dam. He was a strange mixture of vigour, diffidence, and single-mindedness.

'Brass-necked bitches. They didn't know what they did want. And they didn't know what they didn't want, until they didn't want it.'

That brought the house down. It did us all good, not the least Kenworthy. And the talk began to flow again.

'No, Mr Kenworthy, it's as someone just said. While there were uniforms about, they didn't want us. The Major from the Battery had to go down to the school and appeal to the headmistress to keep them away from the perimeter wire.'

'Yes,' Kenworthy said. 'And it was the same thing, wasn't it, when it came to playing a trick on Sally Mason? They did what many a General Officer Commanding has had to do in a tight corner. They called on the Royal Regiment of Artillery. But gentlemen, I ask you: do you think that the Royal Artillery is going to play along with a stunt like that? Knowing, as every man-jack of them must have known, that the man involved was an unknown one-pipper from his own arm of the service? Every one of them counting down the days to his next leave, his next weekend pass? Was there a squaddy on the guns who wouldn't have told those girls to go and get stuffed?'

I was not quite sure what sort of squaddy Kenworthy had been himself in his time, but he knew enough about the background to carry the point with these men.

'So just for once in their darling young lives, they had to turn to the coarse young locals, didn't they? Someone who didn't yet know a second lieutenant from a Sally Army trumpeter? Easy, wasn't it? All he had to do was deliver a note. Oh, and get it back afterwards. Especially important to make sure of getting it back. Even if he had to run for it and lose his knife in the process.'

Kenworthy didn't look in the direction of Cantrell and Lovelock. Nor was there any great sign that his narrative had stirred much up in the others. Maybe there was indeed little in it that was news to them: except perhaps the fact that Kenworthy was on to it.

'Not much of a story, gentlemen, I know. Or maybe I've missed something out. Let's try another one, shall we? Let's talk about one of the other girls – one who wasn't at all like the rest of them. One who talked a lot. One who took things to heart rather. One who could be a bit of a menace, if ever she got an idea into her head. She was a poet too – of a sort. And by that, I don't mean that her poetry was no good; I mean it was something very personal to herself. Like rewriting Shakespeare, bits of him, anyway, to try to make it fit in with what was happening to her. Like

Nurse, oh my love is slain, I saw him go
Over the white Alps alone.

'She didn't write that. Nor did Shakespeare.'

I don't think there'd ever been much poetry declaimed in the Three Horseshoes. But Kenworthy held his audience as if it was poetry they had come here to listen to. He spoke the words quietly and deliberately, and there was something spine-tingling about them in that shabby, silenced bar, with its beer-mats and dartboard and yellow worn dominoes.

'She remembered those lines, and wrote them down – like she remembered other things and wrote them down – when it suddenly dawned on her that there was every likelihood that she was going to be killed herself.'

Lovelock and Cantrell were now as deeply attentive as any man in the room.

'So what made her think that someone might want to kill her? I'll tell you that, too. When she was here as a girl, she wasn't much in league with that mob down in the Powder Mill. When she heard the joke that was to be played on Sally Mason, she set out to stop it. She went out – before any of the others – before you, even, Peter Lovelock, that morning – to paint a sunrise. What she saw gave her a rough idea as to who'd killed the girl. But she wasn't sure. Not sure until last week.'

Kenworthy's glass was still four-fifths full. He glanced down at it, but hardly seemed to see it.

'She came here to get married, and whether she actually would have got married or not need not trouble us for the moment. She went out to call on the one person with whom she might have talked about the old days, saw that she was a reasonably happy housewife in mid-family life, and decided to leave her out of things. But then something else happened; and she knew. And she knew that it was dangerous knowledge.'

He took a short pull at his drink, made a wry face and pushed the mug away.

'That's all, gentlemen. Another pretty rotten story, I know. Something missing somewhere, did you say? Yes, by God, there is.'

He pulled on his coat, beckoned me with his head and walked to the door. But we did not go out. He turned with one hand on the latch and hurled another speech at them. Their eyes were fixed on him with an almost sullen refusal to betray emotion.

'I almost forgot the main thing. That book – the one that doesn't agree with Tuppy Ibberson's story. She wrote that. Under a false name. And I'm sorry to say there are bits in it which we think she made up. That stuff about the naval lieutenant making a quarterdeck confession. We think she probably invented it. But if she did, it wasn't because she was a liar. It was because she was a poet – of a sort. Of the sort that likes things to happen the right way. And that doesn't like history to be unfair to people. Maybe she didn't consider it fair that all those rough old buggers should have been hanged, all those years ago. Perhaps she thought that a bunch of rough young buggers were being blamed for the 1940 crime – and that that wasn't fair, either – '

He paused.

'*There are a thousand paths to the delectable tavern of death, and some run straight and some run crooked.* That's another thing she wrote down. And whose path to death did run straight, gentlemen, and whose run crooked? Mary Boothroyd's? Sally Mason's? Julie Wimpole's? What was it that Julie Wimpole knew – was so sure about for the rest of her life – until last week, when she found out something that changed her mind for her?'

There was no response. He was not expecting any.

119

All he wanted was to leave them thinking – talking about it –

'I think,' he said, 'that while she was on her way across the fields that morning, with her paint-box and her easel, she saw that second lieutenant. She knew that, like Walter Chapman in his day, he had come back.'

CHAPTER TWELVE

We were both ready for bed, but Kenworthy was convinced that something would shortly turn up as a result of his performance in the pub, so he asked me to go over to his lodgings with him. For some considerable time we did not talk. He sat at his table, ruled tabular lines on a sheet of paper, and referred at intervals to a sheaf of voluminous notes, which I had had no idea he had been keeping. He must have worked into the small hours every night we had been here. I had nothing to read but this morning's paper: a demarcation dispute on Clydeside and a pub shoot-out in Finsbury Park.

'Where do you want to go tomorrow, Shiner?'

'Tomorrow?'

It sounded like an open invitation.

'We're going to have to try to dig something out of the War Office, though I doubt whether the sort of records they keep are going to provide any quick answers. Then there's that headmistress: she may be still alive, even possibly still in command of her faculties. Some of the girls might be run to earth, if we look round enough corners. Then there's Halliton-cum-Stansby.'

'I'll settle for Halliton,' I said.

'Wise boy. That's where I'd be myself, if it wasn't the prerogative of old age to stay at home and play the big cheese.'

In point of fact, I thought we had left Halliton more than a trifle lamely, with loose ends still hanging. The youth Caley had dropped his bombshell about Dugdale's knowledge of Julie's presence in Peak Low, but we had not been able to follow this up, because the probation chief had departed for Preston, where he had a case at Quarter Sessions. We had spent the afternoon in the town police station, talking about Harbutt's record, without finding anything new, and arranging for some discreet enquiries into his recent movements. Then Kenworthy had started itching to be back in the hills.

Seeing that he was not apparently ready to talk again, I risked taking him to task for some of the lines he had taken in the pub. To my mind, he had made it too complex.

'Not complex at all. Take the story apart, and it wouldn't rate highly as a jigsaw.'

'But all that literary stuff, about what she might or might not have put into her pamphlet – '

'All right: you say "might or might not". "Might or might not" includes *might* – and if she did, she did it with a purpose: because she wanted to keep the record straight, as she saw it. Not that that's my main concern for the moment. What I most wanted to do was to upset that lot in the pub. I wanted to worry one or two of them even more than they're worried already. If I'm not much mistaken, one or two of them are at this moment agreeing how much to come and tell us. And now – tomorrow . . . '

I was to go back to Halliton to check Harbutt's

alibis. We did not yet know what they were, but he wasn't the type to have left his flanks unguarded. Then I was to see George Dugdale and make him at least uncomfortable for keeping vital facts to himself.

'Not that I think you'll find there's much in it,' Kenworthy said. 'It will probably boil down to his having a wife who doesn't much care for his interest straying.'

And then I was to see the lad with the Standard Eight again. He had been one of Julie's more successful cases. That sort of influence was only achieved by both sides getting to know each other fairly well, so he might have more light to shed. Moreover, he might be the one to tell us whether George Dugdale's interest had strayed or not.

'After all, you never *know*,' Kenworthy said, in a mock-conspiratorial tone that made me wonder if he was thinking of putting it all down to Dugdale after all. Though, yet again, that might be just the sort of line he would shoot when sending a junior out on a time-waster.

I didn't have a chance to follow this up, because at that moment there was a click of the garden gate and discreet footsteps approached the front door. Kenworthy signed to me to be butler, and I brought him in Cantrell and Lovelock.

If they were the flash boys of Peak Low, the evening had reduced them to their essential shoddiness. There had to be something about a local couple who stuck to the lounge, even though they had it to themselves. There was something about Lovelock's herringbone greatcoat, its lapels turned up about his cheeks against the drizzle, that it made it look a good deal less opulent than when he had first bought it off its peg. There was something about the droplets of moisture settled in

Cantrell's hair that made him look less of a ladies' man. Local boys who had stayed in the district: doing jobs far enough away from the village to impress? Ledger-clerks, posing as accountants? Storemen, pretending they were technical consultants? It was easy to see why Kenworthy had given them no quarter. They'd worked hard to elevate themselves in other people's estimation, but the only ones with whom they had succeeded were themselves. Kenworthy left them for a minute or two still frying in their own embarrassment.

'Mr Kenworthy, you've been pretty rough with us, and, well, we didn't really know, you see, that what little bit we'd had to do with it was all that important.'

'We didn't actually commit any *crime*, Mr Kenworthy.'

'You knew there was something you had to keep dark,' Kenworthy said.

'Nobody wants to get involved,' Cantrell argued, preferring a general statement to a personal admission.

'I would have thought that the opposite was true, as far as Peak Low is concerned.'

'I don't know what you mean.'

He made himself sound sweetly reasonable, eager indeed to turn this into a rational discussion. Cantrell was eager to show that as far as he was concerned, all hatchets ought to be buried. He'd gladly talk now. But they did not try to drive any bargain with Kenworthy. I was glad we were spared that.

'I mean that the reason Peak Low won't talk is because no one wants to involve the other chap. It isn't themselves that men are trying to protect – it's each other. Because no one is sure what really happened. Except you two.'

'We don't know what happened. We only know –

but it's no use waffling all round it. We'll have to begin at the beginning.'

'Do.'

'There were these girls from the school, you see.'

'Can you remember their names?'

'There was Doris, Doris Hislop. She was the one with the government paper. A bit of a drip, that one, but she wouldn't let them have a sheet unless they'd let her in on the game. Then there was Brenda. I can't remember her other name. She was yours, if you remember, Pete.'

Lovelock seemed more than naturally annoyed at the suggestion. Perhaps it was because Cantrell's attempt to introduce a joke into the account was such a dismal failure.

'That was what *you* said.'

'Stop a minute,' Kenworthy said. 'How old were you?'

'I was fourteen. Pete was – how old would it be, Pete? Nineteen.'

'Significant difference. And what were you hoping to get out of it?'

'I'll tell you what I was hoping to get out of it,' Lovelock said. 'Sod-all. We weren't exactly sex-maniacs, you know. We only talked as if we were. And the girls didn't even talk about it, in front of us. They just sniggered at odd remarks that didn't mean anything to us.'

'Half a second. We haven't got all their names down yet.'

'There were three, all told: Doris and Brenda and Rowena. Rowena Fitzhugh. She was the one I fancied.'

'You were wasting your time,' Lovelock said. 'And in any case, we'd both have had to stand and whistle for it. They weren't quite St Trinian's types, Mr Kenworthy, but that bloke who draws the cartoons knows what he's doing.'

'Why don't you get on?'

'When you come to size it all up, there's not all that much to get on with. We happened to meet this bunch. In fact, we followed them round four fields, up round the old kilns, and finally caught up with them by Batcher's. That's a disused quarry on the Sparrowpit side. It's true that they didn't want much to do with us as a rule, but we weren't the sort to stop trying. And it's clear enough, looking back, they were stringing us on that afternoon. It never occurred to us, what you said earlier this evening, that they'd tried to get some of the troops involved. But, come to think of it, that makes sense all along the line. Well, we caught up with them in this old quarry, where they'd conveniently stopped for a rest. So we sat down with them.'

'You, Jack? You took fright. You kept trying to edge away.'

'I only wanted to sneak off for a pee. To cut a long story short – '

'Thank God for that,' Kenworthy said.

'They told us about this silly caper they wanted to play.'

'Wait, wait, wait. Which of them spun you the yarn?'

'Rowena. Rowena Fitzhugh. She was the moving spirit, no doubt about that. Moved my spirit, too, she did. Off-blonde; wearing a school hat that she'd taken the band off, and tried to batter into some sort of fashionable shape. Make-up about a quarter of an inch deep, and green pendants that she stuck in her ears the moment she was out of the Powder Mill gates.'

'Obviously your critical senses have picked up a bit since,' Kenworthy said.

'Yes, well, I wouldn't have minded meeting Rowena Fitzhugh again, say ten–twelve years ago.'

'You didn't stay in touch with her?'

'God, no. The way things turned out, I only set eyes on her once after that. And that was when she handed me the note.'

'So get on with the prank you were to play.'

'Well, for some reason, they really seemed to have it in for this girl Sally Mason. I think it was mainly because she was different from them. I don't really know, because I never met her. I'd seen her about. I'd heard people talk about her. A couple who come here to get married is a talking point in every house in the village. She was more grown up than they were. She was getting married, so that made her grown up. She was happy. *They* said she was self-satisfied. They told her to her face that they didn't believe she'd ever set eyes on the man again. It was jealousy, and I didn't know it then, but I know it now, they were jealous because she was the very opposite of all they were trying to be. She was unsophisticated, plain – and bomb-happy.'

'So you delivered the note?'

'They were going to write it, and it was to be signed with an illegible scrawl, supposed to be by some officers' mess friend of the second lieutenant. They knew a lot about what went on in officers' messes – or thought they did. The note was going to say that Johnny Kirkland – that was this officer's name – had had his marriage leave stopped because of operational contingencies. They were proud of that phrase.'

'Just a minute. You said his name. Did *they* know his name? Because no one else did – and it never seems to have come to light till this moment.'

'Oh, they'd wormed it out of Sally Mason, teasing

her, one afternoon up in the hills. They plagued her till she'd have told them anything to be rid of them.'

'And you two thought fit to suppress it till now?'

I had seen Kenworthy in simulated rage. Now I saw him in a real one. If his right hand had splintered the arm of his chair, I would not have been surprised.

'Has it never occurred to you two stupid sods how many people's personal history might have been different, if someone in authority could have got hold of that officer's name?'

'Inspector, don't shoot us down in flames. We were only kids at the time.'

'Kids? Nineteen, did you say? There were men leading platoons into action at nineteen.'

'Inspector, we've sat on this truth for seventeen years. And I don't know what you can do to us for it, but we're telling you now, aren't we? Surely you can see how it was. All I was going to do was to make myself look uncouth and pretend I was going to attack her – '

It was Lovelock who had taken up the narrative now, talking with that desperate vigour of a man who is using every shred of his will-power in an effort to be believed.

'A woman was murdered. And I didn't do it. I didn't even get within sight of her to put on that stupid bloody act. That was what I was going to have to try to explain. Do you think that anyone would have believed me? I was nineteen, I'd never been out of Peak Low in my life. I could see myself being strung up for it, if anyone had connected me. I've got an idea that the girls did think I'd done it. I bet if you could find them now, and ask them, they'd still say it was me. So least said, soonest mended. All I'd got on my conscience was a practical joke that never even got going. And that has been bad enough.'

Kenworthy seemed to have made an effort to subside.

'Did Julie Wimpole think it was you, too?'

'She must have wondered.'

'All right. Let's hear the rest of it.'

Lovelock looked at Cantrell. He preferred his friend to have the telling of it.

'My job was to deliver that letter. Story-book stuff. I was to get up to Ada Bramwell's at first light and chuck gravel up, hoping I was aiming at the right window. And I nearly didn't go, at that. There were no flies on Ada Bramwell – there are none now, come to that. And if she'd copped me at it, and told my dad, it would have been a right belting in the wash-house for me. Then I thought, if I don't do my bit, and Pete's out of bed at this hour of the morning for nothing, that's another bloody good belting from a different quarter. But it didn't come to that. It was a beautiful morning – I suppose. But I wasn't in much of a mood for May flowers and cuckoos. I wanted to get my part of it over, and join the girls, on the rocks over Drydale, from where they were going to watch.'

He was leaning forward in his chair, trying to jerk the conviction of truthfulness into every movement of his hands and arms.

'I got up to Ada Bramwell's, and thanked God that Sally Mason was already awake, looking out of her window. I caught her eye. I waved the note at her. I put it down between two stones. And I pissed off out of it. A few minutes later, hiding in a hollow, I saw Sally Mason in a light summer frock, making her way down to Drydale. I went across country to where the girls had said they were going to be. And they didn't show up. That's all I had to do with it. You'd better tell your part of it yourself, Pete.'

'Yes, well, I'd wanted sod-all to do with it myself. If it hadn't been for letting you down, Jack, I'd have chucked it in. That's how these things start. The girls had suggested that I should put on my oldest clothes. They'd even given me a stump of old lipstick to paint streaks of blood down my face. And they'd cut me a piece of orange peel to stick under my upper lip to look like vampire's teeth. I threw that away before I even got home the afternoon before. But I did set off for Drydale. And I suppose I would have got there. I suppose I'd have done what they wanted, which was to hide up in the shell of that old shepherd's hut and spring out when Sally Mason arrived, expecting to find her boy-friend. I'd have been pretty half-hearted about it, I can tell you. I've never had any talent for that sort of poncing about. The chances are I'd have bust out laughing. But anyway, I was saved all the trouble.'

He looked at Kenworthy with a huge appeal to reason.

'That's another reason why we decided to keep our mouths shut. It would have made no difference to Sally Mason whether Jack and I had been out that morning or not. I hadn't got far down Drydale when there was a bloke in uniform telling me to go back. He said some of the troops from the camp were having an exercise with live ammunition, and it wasn't safe to go any further.'

And a certain twist of satisfaction now came into Lovelock's face.

'And this is where, Inspector, I'm afraid you made a mistake. It wasn't a second lieutenant that Julie Patterson – as she then was – saw. It was the gunner who'd been flogging the knives about the village.'

'He was the one who warned you back?'

Lovelock nodded.

'And what makes you think Julie saw him?'

'At the top of Drydale, there's a little bridge.'

'We know it.'

'As I'm coming up out of the valley, Julie is crossing the bridge. She's hot and flustered and panting, and she's carrying a haversack and a folded flat box. I know now that that was some sort of easel. I told her not to go any further, because of what the soldier had told me. "Live ammunition?" she said. "It must have got bloody damp, then." That's what she said, bloody damp. "Or else they're using bloody good silencers."'

'So there was no stopping her?'

'Well, I argued with myself, she'll be turned back by the sentry. I thought all along that he was a genuine sentry.'

Kenworthy said nothing for some seconds. Then he looked at Cantrell.

'And you saw nothing of this soldier?'

'No.'

'Nor of any other soldiers?'

'No.'

'Nor of Julie Patterson?'

'No.'

'And neither of you has ever said a word of this to a soul?'

'Not till tonight.'

Kenworthy shut his eyes.

'Pity,' he said at last. 'Nothing you did or said could have made any odds to what happened to Sally Mason. But you did sentence Julie to death.'

CHAPTER THIRTEEN

It was one of those nights when I thought there was going to be too much brain-bashing for sleep. But somehow I drifted into an unconsciousness that was dreamless if unrestful. I was wholly unrefreshed when Kenworthy came scratching the panels of my bedroom door before first light.

'Sorry about this, Shiner, but there's something I need to see again. And you need to see it, too.'

It was an appalling morning, if morning it could yet be called, no intimation of grey from the horizon in any quarter. At some time during the night – to judge from the depth of the puddles, it must have been early rather than late – the drizzle had found its true identity as a relentless downpour. Headlamps emerged from the drive of one of the cottages and water splashed hub-high as the driver bent over in mid-turn to fiddle with something on his vacant passenger-seat: a commuter making a raw early start.

We trod the footpath that I was beginning to think I had known all my life: the field track to Drydale. At stiles and gateways the ground was a morass. My foot-wear seemed made of some stylishly reinforced paper. But by the time we reached the landmark footbridge, some sort of substitute for daylight was at last beginning to prevail. I could actually see Kenworthy now, a mixture of dejection and resolution in a drenched trench-coat, the brim of a felt hat pulled down at an angle from which a steady trickle was pouring down on to the handrail. The stream beneath us seemed to have risen a foot and a half in the night. Where I had watched a fallen leaf skirt boulders in the current, it was now only the tips of the larger stones that protruded from the spate. The flood was fast, turgid – and cruel.

'It must have rained like hell,' I said.

'It doesn't have to, to achieve this, Shiner. Now you can see why they call it Drydale.'

In fact, when we had last seen the valley, it was its sterility that had impressed us: down its centre an irregular scattering of stones, that people told us marked the bed of a dried-out river, but that looked in fact more like the debris of a broken wall. But now there were stretches of visible brook, torrents cascading over waterfalls into standing pools, only to disappear again for unpredictable spells.

'Another day or two of this weather, Shiner, and it will be one uninterrupted river. Once the water-table overflows, there are gullies adding their pay-load from both sides. The whole complex is porous; that comes from the chemical properties of the lime. Look on the map, and there's a village over the next hill that's actually called Waterswallows.'

A sound little lesson in geology on a damp bridge on a filthy morning. Kenworthy turned his head and water streamed down from the brim of his hat at a new angle.

'Sorry, Shiner, but we're going to have to get wetter and dirtier still.'

And he led the way down into the valley, a terrible walk, since the place was so seldom ever trodden. There was no beaten footpath and where, on our previous visit, we had picked our way among the stones of the stream-bed, this was now only possible at intervals that became rarer as we lost height, and the waters were ever growing from fresh tributaries.

'Remember we're being watched, Shiner.'

Steep, scree-ridden slopes towered above us on either

side, topped by parapets of weathered rock over which eyes could have been surveying us from a thousand different crannies.

'You can be assured that someone knows we're out – and can't bear not to know what we're on. So, whatever you want to look at, don't betray any interest. Just take it all in – but let's leave them guessing.'

I was doing some systematic conjecture myself. Certainly if Kenworthy had so far spotted anything to justify this excursion, he was successfully concealing it from me. We picked our way along the steep, slippery and uneven watercourse and rain dripped with rhythmless persistence through the branches of the occasional trees. Once Kenworthy spoke back to me over his shoulder.

'Amongst other things, we're looking for the kind of spot where Harbutt is supposed to have been standing, turning back spectators from a non-existent military exercise. Somewhere like this, do you think?'

We were descending a gradient of something like one in five, and at a point some seventy yards below us the valley swung round at a sharp angle to our right, the crest of one hillside overlapping the other like a line of grotesquely denuded crenellations.

'A commanding spot. A man could hold this pass single-handed, given certain prerequisites.'

And as if to confirm the likelihood that this was the place, the rounding of the next bend did in fact bring us within sight of the shepherd's hovel. If Harbutt had stood his sentry-go there, he could in fact have shielded curious eyes from what was happening at the ruin; or, more probably, could have delayed discovery of what had already happened there.

'We could of course ask Lovelock to be more precise,' I said.

'And you will be putting it to Harbutt later this morning.'

We went down as far as a point just below the ruin, which the river skirted in a curve. Downstream from there, there were no more interruptions in the water-course that we could see. Kenworthy clambered along the bank for another twenty yards or so and then came back. We did not play any charades, nor did we approach the ruin itself.

'She drew a picture of this,' Kenworthy said. 'There was a sketch of it in her note-book. You and Parbold seemed to think, in your conversation last night, that it was a preliminary for some future work of art.'

'It was certainly pretty rough,' I said. 'Perfunctory, in fact.'

'I don't agree. I've got it in my pocket, but I don't want to bring it out in this deluge. Or make a present of it to the unseen watcher. It was inartistic, yes. But mark this spot carefully, Shiner. Take a mental photograph of it. I think you will find that that drawing was remarkably exact, even down to individual stones.'

He said no more about it, but on our way back up the valley, unbelievably worse than our descent because the rain was now driving into our faces, he started another theme over his shoulder. It was a fight to ensure any sort of continuity of comprehension, rather like trying to carry on a philosophical discussion on the bridge of a windjammer in a typhoon. The best I can do is to relate it as if it had been a sensible, continuous monologue in warm, dry and silent surroundings.

'I'm warming even more to this young lady, you know, Shiner. She had admirable qualities, one or two of which we could do with in a few of our colleagues. Seventeen years' staying power, for example. And the ability to wait for things to materialise round concealed

134

turnings. I mean: let's suppose she really was in love with Harbutt. Do you think that the final decision, to marry him or not, might have depended on her ability to prove that he didn't kill Sally Mason? Or, on the other hand, might she have gone through the whole love-and-ready-to-marry gambit for the sole purpose of proving that he did? That's something else you can bear in mind while you're chatting up Harbutt. Because, you see, I keep coming back to her underwear. I still can't believe that there was a thing in her suitcase that suggests a girl who's really planning to get married out of it. But I may be wrong about this. Maybe a St Michael's tag turned him on. Or perhaps this was another of her little touches of superstition. Perhaps she thought she might be tempting providence and dis-illusion if she came too well prepared. I've written to my wife about her trousseau. Let's hope there's an answer in this morning's post.'

There were times when Kenworthy tempted the adjective *sweet*. And this chunk of reasoning, as I say, was blown back at me on arrows of cold rain, with shouts for repetition of key phrases, bits of it un-doubtedly misheard or altogether missed. I did not draw abreast with him until we reached the bridge, when I saw that despite our battering, and the struggle of talking in the face of the elements, he was actually laughing.

The early bus was waiting at the cross-roads as we arrived back in the village. The queue of clerks and accountants from the Quarries, with a salting of burly rock-tearers, was shuffling in humbly natural discipline up to the folding doors. Will Beard was amongst them, but appeared quite friendless.

'Change of raiment, Shiner, breakfast – then Halliton.'

'Sir.'

CHAPTER FOURTEEN

I had not expected the sort of reception that I got from
Harbutt – but it was a recognisable attitude. He
decided that I was too junior to be handling one of his
distinction; I let it flow over me. He knew well enough,
without being reminded, what the score really was. But
Harbutt, reformed or not, had a lifetime of orthodox
crime behind him; there were certain behaviour
patterns that easily claimed him. Moreover, he was
aggrieved, and he said so, not without a nominal
measure of justification, though he knew as well as I did
that he was wasting his time. It was bad for him to be
interviewed at his place of work. But I had no choice,
if I was to get my day's work done.

He had a job on an assembly-line, obtained for him
by the Probation Office's fund of good-will. I was given
the use of a foreman's office, a cubicle of green metal in
a corner of a machine-shop. Our best hope of confiden-
tiality came from the clatter all round us.

'I've come for your alibi,' I said. 'I believe Kenworthy did mention it to you in passing.'

'And he also mentioned it to the local jacks,' Harbutt
said bitterly.

He enumerated his items on the fingers of his left
hand.

'Last Thursday night, till a quarter past midnight, in
a pub whose name it really wouldn't be fair to mention
– though I will if I'm actually charged. Then home
with a dolly-bird; likewise protected until the last
ditch. I left her at half past five. Not very helpful, is
it?'

'A dolly-bird, the same week as you were supposed to be marrying Julie?'

'So what do you say to that, Sergeant? Tut-tut? I've already told you how I mixed it all up with Julie. I don't want to have to go into that again.'

As previously with Harbutt, I was disconcertingly conscious of a tone of possible sincerity, a hint of weariness of the spirit that it might have been beyond the power of the man to act. But how could one be sure of anything with Harbutt? I made slow, unnecessarily verbatim notes. Harbutt watched me with provocative cynicism.

'I'm glad you've got all that down, Sergeant. Make sure you put it just like that to Kenworthy.'

It was all part of the act, to take sides with a sergeant against his superior.

'It will impress him a lot more, Sergeant, than something all neatly sewn up. I don't even have to try, do I?'

'Maybe not. And I don't doubt that Kenworthy will be glad to see his options open.'

'Let's leave that to Kenworthy, shall we?'

'You're a cheeky bugger, Challis. Mind if I still call you that? Julie must have had lingering doubts.'

'About what?'

'About whether you killed Sally Mason.'

'Why should she think that?'

'Because you were there.'

'There? Where?'

'In the valley,' I said. 'Guarding the defile. Cock and bull story about troops on manoeuvre.'

I could see that this affected him. It did not rattle his show of self-confidence, but it gave him to think. In his normal bravado, he would have asked me outright for my source. But he didn't. He was trying to work it out for himself.

'Under orders,' he said.

'Whose orders?'

'I never did get to know his name. A second lieutenant, R.A. Came pelting past me just as I was crossing the dale – I came down one side and up the other, you know, quickest way back to camp. And he said to me, "Gunner," he said, "You stand here for the next quarter of an hour. Don't let anyone a step further down the valley than this. Tell them there's a stunt on, with live ammunition." '

If this was opportunism on Harbutt's part, he was even quicker – and luckier – than I had given him credit for.

'Now take it easy,' I said. 'What time of day was this?'

'A few minutes to five, ack emma.'

'Gone down to listen to the cuckoo, had you?'

'No. Sleeping out. Unofficial, you know. Bags of perimeter wire and all that.'

'One of the girls from the school, was it?'

'Do me a favour.'

'I shall have to know, Challis.'

He looked at me with over-acted pity. But this time he *was* over-acting.

'There's no need to go stirring her up, Sarge. She's probably got fifteen grown-up kids by now. There's no telling what trouble you might stir up for her.'

'You should have thought of that at the time.'

'Well, I'll say the same as I did over the alibi: till the last ditch.'

'This is the last ditch. You can tell me now, or I'm taking you in to help.'

'You wouldn't want the trouble.'

'I'd love it.'

'Honestly, Sergeant. I don't think I can remember.'

For a second I thought he was going to defeat me

with temporary amnesia, real or feigned. But he struggled with his memory. Harbutt did not want to be held for questioning. He would have found it too reminiscent.

'Try Aggie Heathcote,' he said. 'Her old man was away on a mine-sweeper, or something. And may God forgive you and me both.'

'Thank you,' I said. 'So now we've got you down in Drydale just at the moment when a second lieutenant is passing. How did he look: scared, angry, passionate?'

'In a hell of a hurry.'

'That all?'

'That's all I can tell you.'

'And how many people did you actually turn back?'

'Two.'

'Tell me.'

'First it was one of the local hoy-boys. Looked like something out of a swede-basher's dole-queue. He went back without any second telling.'

'Go on.'

'Well, then it was Julie.'

There was something hangdog about the way he said that. And it all fitted in with what we had heard from Cantrell and Lovelock. I even began to wonder if there had been overnight consultation.

'So Julie,' I said, 'must have wondered ever after if you'd done the killing.'

'No. She knew very well I hadn't.'

'How?'

'She was with me, grappling hand to hand, when we heard the scream.'

'Whose scream?'

'Sally Mason's, I suppose. It was only round the next corner of the dale.'

'So you went running?'

'Up, not down. Bags of mind my own business. I wasn't supposed to be out of camp.'

'Not exactly a paragon of public spirit in those days, either, were you?'

'Never have been, Sarge. I mean, I'd just done something to oblige a strange officer. You'd always do that, as long as it cost you nothing. It had crossed my mind that I might somehow use him to cover up for me. My time was running thin.'

'So Julie ran straight down the dale?'

'Not straight away. I'll tell you how it was. She'd come down the valley, carrying all this kit with her – a great flat box, nearly too awkward to handle. I told her she wasn't to go any farther, and she started to argue with me. I told her she was likely to get caught in the cross-fire, but she didn't believe me. Then she tried to dash past me, and I got hold of her by the hands, and we started wrestling. I was having a bit of fun, really.'

'Clearly.'

'Then we heard the scream, while we were still mucking about. She said something about being too late now, and the poor kid was going to be scared out of her wits.'

'But you knew all along that it must be murder?'

'No. I just thought the one-pip wonder had bitten himself off one that was proving hard to get.'

'And Julie? How long did you hold on to her?'

'Two minutes? Less: it was like fighting a tigress. She'd dropped her easel and it had come partly unfolded. She was in a muck-sweat trying to fix it. Then she slipped on a stone and dropped it again.'

'But she did go down the valley?'

'Eventually.'

'How long, then, between her hearing the scream and coming upon the body?'

'I can't say for certain. A good five minutes.'

'And you didn't go down after her?'

'No. I hared back to camp. Overdue.'

For the second time, I was glad to have slow notes to write.

'So by and large, you'd say Julie thought the officer was the murderer? You must have talked that over with her dozens of times.'

'Not dozens of times. We let once do for all. Yes: that's what she did think. But she'd no proof of it. There was no sign of the officer when she got there, which was why she kept her mouth shut. She said she wasn't providing circumstantial evidence that could lead to a wrongful conviction. She talked like that, even in those days.'

'But she pointed the way, didn't she?'

'How do you mean?'

'She published a bit of doctored history that might have made anyone think – who was capable of thinking.'

'I don't know anything about that. It sounds far-fetched to me.'

'It beats me,' I said, 'how you kept yourself out of the hands of the investigation.'

'I didn't. I was in their hands. They were worried because I couldn't produce my knife. Bloody funny, that, because I'd handled three dozen knives, the previous week.'

'And you managed to keep all the rest of the story dark?'

'Too bloody true, I did. The trouble is, Sarge, you and I don't live in the same world.'

'You want to try mine, sometime, Challis.'

And I found myself wondering inanely whether St Michael's tags really did turn him on.

CHAPTER FIFTEEN

I was going to lose no sleep for having cast suspicion on James Harbutt by interviewing him at his place of work. But Matthew Caley was a different proposition. The first time we had met him, he had been brought from his work-bench to the Probation Office: a young man 'going straight' in a job fixed for him by the inner wheel of social do-goodery. Kenworthy had put him last on my day's list: there were a dozen ways in which I could have caused him to side-step on his way home after the afternoon buzzer. But it seemed to me now an urgency that Kenworthy would not question, to squeeze Caley flaccid of anything he had to tell me before I closeted myself with Dugdale.

So I went to the small electronic sub-contractor's workshop that had been set up in the shell of an abandoned Methodist Chapel, and better than Harbutt's foreman's cubicle, was accorded temporary use of a female rest-room; with the understanding that I might have to surrender to some mob-capped, green-overalled period pain at very short notice. I perched with my legs swinging on the edge of a leather inspection couch, inhospitable enough to get all but the hard cases back to their soldering irons in an average of twenty minutes. I put Caley, with more than a hint of even colder formality in reserve, on a folding chair at a table where I could look down on him.

'So. What have you thought of since we last met, that you now feel we ought to know?'

Like Harbutt, he was angry at being sent for again — but for different reasons.

'Look, Sergeant, what I told you before was supposed to be in confidence. I'd promised Mr Dugdale – '

So Dugdale had already been on to him? Interesting.

'I know nothing that could possibly be any use to you,' Caley said.

A Juvenile Delinquent: the term meant something very different in the Probation Office from what it meant in the public bar of the *Three Horseshoes*; and something different again, I'd no doubt, in the crowded C.I.D. office and Edwardian charge-room of the local nick. Matthew Caley had wiry hair in a crew-cut a fortnight overgrown; he had blue eyes that could hopefully turn on a blend of offended innocence; a mouth that could drop at the corners into surly truculence at the moment of seeing himself trapped; a rather feminine pointed chin that I'd no doubt he could see himself setting like the V of a snow-plough in the face of opposition. Kenworthy and I, of course, were not far from cynical about the pervasive optimism of Dugdale and Julie and their kind – though we conceded their right to try. We were even prepared to believe that they sometimes pulled it off.

I looked at Matthew Caley and wondered what methods might have succeeded in his case. Not moral persuasion, certainly; not sentimental religion – he'd probably seen his fill of the products of that; sheer economics, or unembroidered pragmatism, perhaps. Or maybe she had won him over just by being Julie.

'Just let's run over everything you know. Start at the beginning and leave nothing out.'

'I don't know anything. What do you expect me to know?'

'You went to Peak Low – '

'That isn't a bloody crime, is it?'

'Cut out the tough stuff, Caley. There's something

143

about you that it doesn't seem to suit. What did you go to Peak Low for anyway? The off-chance of running into Julie?'

'Sergeant, for God's sake, what is this? You're talking to me as if – '

'As if what, Caley? Let's hear you finish the sentence.'

But he couldn't. The reaction was suggestive – but told me nothing conclusive, though it implied that he might be as sentimental as Julie had often showed herself.

'I'm talking to you as you've been talked to before by the likes of me. Is that what you mean?'

I hadn't planned to be as nasty with him as this. I was playing it a move at a time, and I suppose I recognised him as one you'd get more out of in the long run if you flattened him out first.

'I thought that was all finished with,' he said. 'Nothing's ever finished, with you bastards, is it?'

'No. Nothing. Ever. Because we're concerned with things that actually happen, not with things that might or might not.'

'You can ask anyone you like when I was last in trouble. Ask your oppos in the nick here.'

'I'm not concerned with a joy-ride to Blackpool this time, Caley. This is a murder.'

I watched the shock settle on him. My statement wasn't news to him, but my attitude was. I saw his eyes stray over to the door, look down at the table, then lift themselves to my face, with the firm intention of staring me out if need be. The realisation had come to him that he was shut away, in a remote little room, at the mercy of a wild man capable of practically everything except sympathy or reason.

'Well, for God's sake, you don't think I'd anything to do with that?'

'We haven't ruled anybody out so far.'

Just a small concession to his possible innocence.

'That shows how little you bloody understand, Sergeant.'

He was about to put all the emotional energy he could muster into one enormous appeal – an appeal to logic, justice, fair play, even to the possibility that beneath the copper there might be a remnant of long-forgotten humanity.

'Sergeant, there's just one spot in which I might one day find myself down for murder; and I'd be bloody glad and bloody proud if I were. And that's if I could put my hands on the bastard that did it to Julie.'

'Yes.'

There is nothing quite so pathetic, so heroic, so wholly committed, as the youth who thinks he is – no: let me rephrase that, without trying to soften up the pitiful truth. There is nothing so far gone as the callow youth who *is* in love with an older woman. It was the old syndrome of the psychiatrist's couch. That was how Julie had handled him; and I supposed she'd seen clearly enough what it was she was doing. I didn't think for a moment she'd have risked letting things get out of hand. Straighten him out and let time – or some other girl, in due course – do the rest of the healing.

There were tears not very far behind his voice.

'If you knew what I owed to Julie.'

'All right, lad. Tell me then. Why you went to Peak Low. What you saw there. And what you thought about it.'

'We went to Peak Low for the day out. We go some-where most weekends: the coast, or the Lakes, or the hills.'

'So why Peak Low this particular weekend?'

'Because we'd been to Southport the Sunday before,

and we were going into the Trough of Bowland the Sunday after.'

'You didn't expect to see Julie there?'

'I didn't see her every day of the week, you know, or even every week, for that matter. I didn't even know she was on leave.'

'So you saw her in the pub. Did she catch your eye?'

'No. She spotted us, all right. That was why she got out of it pretty smartly. She didn't catch my eye. If she had, one of the others might have seen her, and it would have been news all over Halliton.'

'So what made you think she didn't want it to be news?'

'The way she made off.'

'And who were your friends?'

'Lads from up and down town.'

'All on Julie's books, were they?'

'No. Mostly straight. Only one beside myself has any form. He's still on weekly report.'

Form. There was something familiar, yet oddly out of place, in the way he liked to show he was at home with the jargon. I wondered whether Julie had been grateful to him for his willingness to be safe company for someone else on her weekly report list.

'So why do you think she was anxious not to be recognised?'

'Fairly obvious, isn't it?'

'What I am trying to get at is, what was obvious to you at the time?'

'That bastard Harbutt.'

'You knew she'd gone to Peak Low to keep a date with Harbutt, did you?'

'I didn't know it, Sergeant: I thought so.'

I felt his reluctance to talk about the subject. He was

146

probably still so jealous of Harbutt that he did not want to face up to the reality of the man.

'You knew all about her and Harbutt, did you?'

'Who didn't? It had been going on for months. Up at pubs over on Belmont. Weekends at Lytham St Anne's.'

'You sound pretty sour about it.'

'I wasn't the only one in Halliton to feel let down. I'm not the only one she helped, you know. There are others who'd be doing bird by now, if it hadn't been for Julie. How do you think we all felt, seeing her swept off her feet by a shyster like that?'

'You knew him fairly well personally, I take it?'

'By reputation. That was reason enough for not wanting to know him any better.'

'But she had him going straight, hadn't she?'

'What does going straight mean? Harbutt is a devious sod. He could afford to play a waiting game.'

'But you find it surprising that Julie was taken in by him? Wouldn't you have said that she was professional, and experienced, and shrewd enough to have seen through him?'

Outside I heard the wheezing electric motor of a milk-float pull into the kerb. Someone pushed open the door of the rest-room, saw us and retreated as if they had been stung.

'We had to accept the obvious facts, hadn't we?'

Caley's tone was both angry and hopeless.

'It didn't cross your mind that she might perhaps have been stringing him along for some purpose of her own?'

'Julie didn't work like that. It's true she didn't always stick to the book. But underneath she was always very – proper's the word for it.'

Proper. There had been hesitation in his search for the

term. Had he on some occasion been too frank about his own feelings for Julie, and had she had to push him down?

'Proper,' I said. 'Doesn't that make it all the less likely that she'd be taken in by Harbutt?'

'She *was* taken in by him. That's what matters, isn't it? There's something about the bastard that's so – I can't think of the word – '

'Plausible? Will that fill the bill?'

'It'll do.'

'What you're really trying to tell me, aren't you, is that you know that Julie had certain weaknesses that made her easy prey for Harbutt?'

'I don't know about weaknesses, Sergeant. She wasn't weak according to my book.'

'But you wouldn't describe her as normal, would you? No; that's not the idea I'm after. She wasn't *ordinary*, was she?'

'Ordinary? Julie? Too true she wasn't.'

'So what was out of the ordinary about her? What would make her fall for Harbutt? After all, you're telling me that you've no doubt that she did fall for him.'

He gave the impression of trying hard to think about it. I don't think he understood, at his stage of life, about falling in love beyond control, without reason, without anything that would stand up to analysis – and with total disregard for prudence, practicalities or local diplomacy; though that was precisely what he'd done himself.

'I would have thought she'd have had more sense,' he said.

'Well, how about sex? Harbutt had a name to live up to, didn't he?'

This, I knew, was sheer cruelty to him. I had the

feeling that Caley was probably still virginal. His knowledge of sex was perhaps not yet out of the dirty-story stage, though maybe it had been sublimated by fresh air and his ludicrously painted banger. I guessed that Julie's carryings on with Harbutt had offended nothing so brutally as his image of her purity.

'Bastard!' was the only response he could rise to.

'So how did you know that Julie and Harbutt had a rendezvous in Peak Low?'

This brought a fresh wave of anger from him.

'I didn't bloody know it. Don't keep coming back at me like that. And stop trying to spring traps on me. I'm giving it to you straight, and if you ask me honest questions, I'll give you honest answers. When I saw her sneak out of the pub, I put two and two together.'

'Had she ever talked to you about Peak Low? In the days when you were one of her cases, I mean?'

'Only as a good centre for an outing. And she'd told me the yarns about the runaway couples.'

'Just as yarns? Or with a personal connection?'

'Personal connection? What personal connection could she possibly have had with what happened all those years ago?'

'And when did you first connect her with a possible runaway marriage?'

'It was old Dugdale who first suggested it, when I told him I'd seen her. He was bloody beside himself. He did his nut.'

'So why was he so angry? Professional considerations? Repercussions in his office? Or because she was buggering up her career?'

'There was that, I suppose.'

I watched his features as he came to a decision.

'And he was soft about her. Everybody knew that. It was the laugh of Halliton.'

And Caley laughed – or tried to. But there wasn't much mirthfulness about it.

'Stupid old bugger! As if he stood a chance with her! But she used to use him. You didn't have to be on the inside to know that. I mean, there were times, everybody knew it, when she went over the limits on the job. If Julie didn't like the rules, she used to find her own way through them.'

He told me a story that I was able to identify as a garbled version of the one Dugdale had told us himself: about how Julie had once stuck her neck out to provide a case-subject with a dubious alibi.

'It was because of that sort of thing that people didn't let Julie down,' Caley said.

'And how long had this been going on, Dugdale's sweetness on Julie?'

'Since ever, I suppose.'

According to our records, Julie had been in Halliton nine years. So how old had Caley been when she first came here? A kid not out of primary school? *Since ever* –

'But to the best of your knowledge, she never gave him any encouragement?'

'Spare us the horrors, Sergeant. I mean, Harbutt, that's physically thinkable, but Dugdale – '

Caley's conception of sex slotted into orthodox and essentially pretty categories.

'I dare say she knew how to smile at him,' he added. 'That would be enough to send Dugdale home happy.'

'Tell me something about his personal life.'

Caley looked at me as if he were searching for something.

'He has a sick wife. That's all part of the picture, part of the general laugh.'

'It's generally considered funny that Dugdale's wife is sick?'

'I don't mean that. I mean, everybody's always said that he'd only got to hang on long enough, and his chance with Julie would come.'

'But you hadn't shared his hopes?'

'What, that dried-out old bugger? And Julie? Have a heart.'

Somewhere in the factory a woman's voice was raised, calling workers to the tea-trolley. I looked closely at Caley and mused on how simple all these issues were to him, how limited his horizon – and how confident his judgement. He said nothing more for some seconds, then evidently made up his mind about something.

'Look, Sergeant, there *is* something I think you ought to know. Only you'll have to promise – '

'No wheeler-dealing, Caley. Not today.'

'Dugdale must never know that I've told you this.'

'This case is eventually going to Assizes, Caley: Q.C.s on both sides. There are no secret clauses in this sort of record. Why are you afraid of Dugdale, anyway?'

'I made him a promise.'

'This is too big a thing for schoolboy honour, Caley.'

'I'm not afraid of Dugdale. It isn't that. I'm in the clear nowadays. I want to stay that way. Dugdale will still be in town when you've disappeared in the dust. I can't afford to be on the wrong side of him. I don't want you pissing in my chips, Mr Wright.'

'No promises, Caley. It'll have to depend on the closing scene. And on Kenworthy's angle on events, not mine.'

He thought for some more seconds.

'It was on the Monday I met Dugdale. He called me in on the Tuesday, said he was going out to Peak Low that night to have it out with Julie once and for all. If

151

there was any sense to be talked into her, it was going to be talked. And there's another thing that wouldn't surprise me. I'll bet he had a good old natter with the jacks to see if they couldn't find something on Harbutt at the last moment.'

'That isn't even hearsay, Caley. It's mere supposition.'

'Sorry, Sarge.'

'But Dugdale's trip to Peak Low – that's *pukka*?'

'*Pukka.*'

'On the Tuesday?'

'That's right.'

What was it the Bagshaw child had said? He was sure it was Tuesday that they had heard the footfall on the stair, because on Tuesday they'd had recorders at school.

'And he did go? You saw him afterwards?'

'No. But I know he went. You see, he asked me if he could borrow my car, and the mileage was on the clock.'

'He borrowed your car?'

'Because he didn't want to take his own for fear of making his wife wonder what he was up to. She thought he was on a conference at Preston, and he would stay overnight. He sometimes did; but he always went by train.'

'Sounds a lame sort of story to me.'

'That's how it was, Sarge.'

CHAPTER SIXTEEN

I had not intended to err on the side of sympathy when I re-opened matters with Dugdale. We were contemptuous about the herd instinct of Peak Low. Up there they kept vital secrets out of adherence to a code that no one could satisfactorily have summarised: loyalty for loyalty's sake, the preference for a crude and ancient allegiance, rather than the clearly acknowledged order of the world that Kenworthy and I served. The men of Peak Low were suffused, as it were, with a team spirit for a side that no longer existed. But Dugdale was a professional man, a kingpin in a hierarchy of social service, albeit a notoriously underpaid one, a leader amongst leaders. Yet he was the first man in the case against whom we could positively accuse compounded deceit. He had kept from us the fact that he had known, for practically the whole of Julie's last week alive, exactly where she was to be found. The nocturnal drive to call on her was unbelievably devious in a man so close to the heart of drab legality. And to have done so in that infamously recognisable car, borrowed from Matthew Caley, had sinister overtones which had not seemed to occur at all to the lad's innocence. It was to be no quarter for George Dugdale. I could picture the memorable rage, histrionic or real, with which Kenworthy would certainly treat this moment.

And I wondered, of course, whether there was not at least an off-chance that time would reveal some tidy little connection between Dugdale and the past. Could he too have had something to do with that Ack-ack battery along the Peak Forest Road? Or perhaps with the school at the Powder Mill? The need to cover exhaustively all possibilities led my imagination along capricious paths that I am sure Kenworthy would have admired.

I lay in wait for Dugdale at the end of his office day – there would be too many interruptions at the top of those lino-covered stairs – and fell in step with him on the pavement as he left the town centre for his middle-class housing estate. I was interested to see Dugdale's home: but taken aback when I did.

It was a spec-built immediate post-war semi, already beginning to look disconsolately inferior in a double row of its peers. Alone in the Avenue, its front lawn was a patchwork of reverted rye-grass and irregular bald channels; the borders showed no evidence that they had borne anything for the summer beyond a few scrawny wallflowers and a profusion of plantains. Dugdale had to use his latch-key: he had to stoop to free the after-noon's mail, jammed between the door and the mat. At once he called upstairs.

'Not up today, dear?'

'I came down to make myself some lunch.'

In the tiny twentieth-century kitchen an empty bean tin still stood on the draining-board.

'If you'll excuse me, I'll make my wife up a tea-tray before we settle down to talk.'

But before the electric kettle came to the boil, she pushed open the kitchen door and joined us: a woman on whom middle age weighed prematurely, hair grey, thin and perfunctorily combed, a beige dressing-gown that seemed almost aggressively shabby, flat-footed slippers prinked with tufts and bobs of synthetic fur that matched nothing else in sight. Dugdale introduced us and she flopped into a kitchen chair and watched him clumsily making toast under the cooker grill.

'This shocking thing about poor Julie.'

She had coarse skin, greasy with some sort of cream that she had smeared on for a day in bed. Dugdale looked at her with what seemed like genuine affection, then caught my eye with a totally unconvincing attempt at a twinkle in his own.

'I keep telling her that she must try to put it out of her head.'

'As if anyone could!'

It seemed an age before we could closet ourselves away from her, but at last Dugdale carried the tray for her into their dining-room, switched on the bar fire and took me upstairs to their smallest, box-room bedroom, which had been hopefully fitted out as an office-study, but had gradually been encroached upon as a repository for white elephants.

'How long have things been like this?' I asked frankly.

'It's been coming on for years. The doctor seems to think that she could do more for herself than she does, and that it would be good for her to try. But what am I supposed to do: bully her? We just have to soldier on.'

'But how do you manage?'

'Somehow; that is, if we *can* be said to manage. It hasn't always been quite as difficult as this. Now you know why I was foolish enough to attempt to lie to you and Kenworthy, rather than to risk any implication of involvement with Julie coming to Elvira's ears. She has always been far more jealous of Julie than circumstances have ever justified.'

He had dropped his voice in an attempt to speak in confidence; somehow the effort seemed absurd. What he knew about acting stances, he must have learned from the stars of the silent cinema.

'I need hardly say,' he added, in the most embarrassing of hoarse whispers, 'that never, not for five minutes, not for thirty seconds, not for five, had she ever had the most slender grounds for suspicion.'

He was far from sure that I believed him, and I chose at first to be silent on the point, which disturbed him more than a direct question might have done. The chance to talk the subject out was the relief he most wanted. I looked at him with disbelief almost as absurdly ham-acted as his own recent bout.

'I must tell you,' he said, 'that I belong to an unofficial group of colleagues who have a monthly meeting of a social nature in a hotel in Preston. We do not take our cars; not that we ever set out with the intention of drinking a glass too many; if we do, it is by accident, as it were, and rare. But we prefer not to inhibit ourselves with the prospect of having to drive home – men in our position. I stay overnight, return by the six o'clock train, and arrive back in time to cook Elvira's breakfast before leaving for the office as if in the normal way. That is where Elvira assumed I had gone that Tuesday evening.'

Men in their position: I found it pitifully easy to believe. Dugdale in his cheap dark suit, with solemn, worried eyes, the beginning of a bottle-nose, saddled with a domestic situation from which there was no way out except his sense of duty, which must necessarily become less and less effective with the passing of the months.

'I see. And what line of argument did you take with Julie?'

'An appeal to reason. Renewed insistence on the character of the man with whom she was infatuated. I must confess that I was living in hope that by some miracle he would still come out in his true colours before the end of her waiting period in Peak Low. I had no faith in his ability to be going really straight.'

'You'd had a word with the local C.I.D., I wouldn't be surprised, in case they had anything hanging fire against him?'

'Very unofficially. There was nothing illegal or underhand, I do assure you, Sergeant.'

'No need to assure me. And there was nothing?'

'Nothing. I have to admit that Harbutt appeared to be behaving like an extremely good boy – ever since he and Julie had taken up with each other.'

'But you were not impressed? And how did Julie receive your unexpected visit?'

'Politely. Even expressing convincing gratitude for my concern. But immovable. Her mind was made up.'

'She did not throw a fit of temper at your intervention?'

'Not this time. She had done so on a previous occasion, but that was uncharacteristic. You did not know Julie, Sergeant.'

He had eyes that were too lustreless to show warmth, but there was a gravity in them that strongly tempted belief.

'I was saying just now, Sergeant, that Elvira had no grounds whatever for suspecting my loyalty. I must qualify that – but only on the level of the thoughts that enter a man's mind. No man can stay his thoughts from straying occasionally into the future.'

If his conscience was indeed as active as he suggested, then he was a man whose mental life must have been a protracted torture.

'Had you ever mentioned such thoughts to Julie?' I asked.

'Only in the vaguest possible fashion; only by innuendo. But that was enough for Julie. I don't try to present her as a mind-reader, but she was astute.'

'And what encouragement did she give you?'

'None whatsoever. No words were spoken. None needed to be. A sad smile, a shake of her head. I must put all such thoughts out of my mind.'

'This was before or after she took up with Harbutt?'

'Before.'

'There was any other great love in her life?'

'The Leading Aircraftman whose head was taken off by an undercarriage. And she was not being faithful to him out of sentimental self-promises. I think it was the fear of invidious comparisons. They had been blissfully happy.'

'How long were you in Peak Low that evening?'

'I was in her room perhaps half an hour. Time for her to make me a coffee. I insisted that I was not going to linger.'

'So you had little chance to talk about anything but the forthcoming wedding?'

'I was coming to that.'

We heard Mrs Dugdale come up the stairs. I half expected her to pause outside the door of the study. And indeed her foot did seem slower and heavier on the landing. But she passed into her bedroom and we heard her close the door.

'When I decided, against my better judgement, to suppress information about this fatuous excursion of mine, the thing that worried me was that there is another piece of information – '

'What, precisely, Mr Dugdale?'

'Julie did say something about the Sally Mason case. Not much – but I could see that it had been occupying her mind – as indeed it had occupied it continuously for years.'

'What did she say?'

'I was left with the impression, though she did not put it into so many words, that she thought she now

158

knew who had killed the second lieutenant's young lady.'

'But she did not tell you? You did not *ask* her, Mr Dugdale?'

'Sergeant Wright, I did not take the Mason case as seriously as Julie did. I had never even really considered it. I was in Peak Low in a last bid to talk her out of a disastrous marriage. It irritated me that she should try to change the subject to something that had long been worn out as a topic of conversation between us.'

'But what did she actually *say*?'

'That it was a funny thing, but she now knew that she had been wrong about it all these years.'

'No more than that? You did not press her for details?'

'Sergeant Wright, my very next remark was, "Julie, I didn't come here to talk about that." '

And that was the sum total of the positive information that he had to tell me. I was aware that things had ended up as a limp parody of the tough line I had intended to take with him. I also knew well enough professionally that whether it is fair treatment or not, there is often much to be learned from watching a man's reaction to hostile interrogation. Moreover, there was something niggling persistently into a corner of my brain. It had been troubling me ever since Caley had told me about Dugdale's trip.

How had he got into Peak Low and into Julie Wimpole's flat without falling into the trap of the hill-folks' eternal vigilance? The suspicions of the Bagshaw children had never had more than rudimentary value as evidence, but they had now gained ground. The footstep they had heard on the stairs must surely have been Dugdale's. But how had he found the staircase to the flat? How had he even found Starvelings – without having to stop to ask someone? There are two normal sources of immediate information about the residents of a village: the Post Office (which would have been closed at that time of night) and the pub. But the pub had been quick to report the arrival of the absurdly painted car on the Sunday; why then so silent about it on the Tuesday night?

I rounded on Dugdale.

'What time did you leave Halliton that night?'

'About a quarter to eight.'

'Did you stop anywhere on the way?'

'Only for petrol. There wasn't enough in the tank for the double journey. And I filled it right up, to give young Matt Caley a bonus.'

'I suppose it was necessary to borrow that ridiculous car?'

'Sergeant Wright, if you knew Elvira! If you knew how she reacts to any variation from normal routine! If she had thought I was motoring to Preston for our monthly get-together –'

'Where did you stop for petrol?'

'An all-night forecourt between Manchester and Stockport.'

'So how long did the journey take you?'

'Two and a half to three hours. At thirty-five miles an hour, that bus is flat out.'

'So what time did you scratch on the panels of Julie's door?'

'About ten to eleven. I looked at my watch.'

'You hadn't lost any time in finding her, then?'

Dugdale grunted, a comical little half-laugh.

'I could regale you with my stumblings. There are no lights in the village. I had not, you understand, the faintest idea of where to start looking. In the end, I knocked at a cottage door for information; but they would not open up to me, although there were lights within.'

'There is a strong sense of privacy in Peak Low. What then?'

'The *Three Horseshoes* was the obvious answer, but I did not want to go into a bar filled with men and face a battery of ribaldry, whilst I compromised Julie by asking for her at that time of night.'

'So?'

'I parked just off the forecourt of the pub and decided that I'd go in, as a casual drinker, and keep my ears open. Then I might be able to have a quiet word with someone discreet – the landlord, perhaps.'

'And is that what happened?'

'No. I was approaching the door when a man came out, evidently on his way round the back to the urinal. I acted on impulse and asked him point-blank, not very consistent of me, you may think, after the way I'd been vacillating. He'd had a fair amount to drink, but I wouldn't describe him as drunk.'

'You asked for Julie outright?'

'No. I tried to be at least a little oblique about it. I spoke of the young lady who had been here for a week or more.'

'And whose description he recognised at once?'

'He gave me the most precise instructions on finding her – including two ways of approaching the farm: one along an intersection of tracks and through the grounds of an old mill; the other round by the road.'

'Which was the one that you took?'

'Obviously.'

'And this man to whom you spoke: can you describe him to me?'

'It was pitch-dark. I was aware of his form, not his features. He spoke with the local accent.'

'So do two or three hundred others. Height? Age?'

'About my height or an inch or two shorter. His age? From his voice? Second half of his life, I would hazard. But nearer than that – '

'Did he stay to see you drive off?'

'No. He told me what I wanted to know, and disappeared round the back with some urgency.'

I went to the patch of waste ground on which Matthew Caley forlornly parked his car, and studied the vehicle. Something told me that it was going to loom large in our field of vision over the next forty-eight hours.

Orange and purple were the basis of the design: diagonal slashes of forked lightning in the former, and irregular blobs of the latter; under both great bubbles of rust and patches of badly applied fibre glass. There was also a recurrent motif of cats in various colours chosen for their general contribution to the cacophonous effect: cats with tails and whiskers, disappearing fragments of tails and whiskers unattached to any visible cat. I did not make a memorandum sketch. I did not need to. After two minutes I could have identified that car in any context.

I stopped for a fill at the obvious all-night forecourt on the Manchester–Stockport road.

'I remember that bloody thing,' the attendant said. He seemed to consider its very existence a personal affront.

'Funny, isn't it, the way things always seem to happen in threes? Three times in the last couple of weeks I've seen that bloody thing.'

'*Three* times?'

'Once on Sunday morning, teeming with noisy buggers. Once one night last week, only that time it was being driven by some bulbous-nosed old fuddy-duddy who ought to have known better than to have it on the road. Then again last Friday – I remember that because it was my last time on nights. Only that time it didn't stop.'

'And who was at the wheel then?'

'I didn't see, mate. I can't say he was speeding, because it couldn't bloody well speed. But he was doing his best.'

'North or south, was he going?'

'South about half past three, north about a quarter past five.'

CHAPTER SEVENTEEN

When I arrived back in Peak Low, the pub was already closed. Kenworthy and I were in no way concerned about licensing hours, and nor, I guess, in the normal run of life, was Bill Hepplewhite. But one spin-off from the presence of the Yard was a wave of general distrust. The curtains of the public bar were thrown open and there was no light in the room. But there was life in the lounge and I thought – hoped, in fact – that Kenworthy might still be at it.

He was. He had to cross the room to open the street door for me, turned as soon as I was in and went back to the table at which he was sitting with Will Beard, Beard's tobacco-tin open in front of him, and a paper protruding from the rollers of his patent machine.

The most striking thing about the pair was their state of relaxation. Kenworthy was still smiling at something that had apparently been said before my entry; it was an interesting smile – the sort of expression of relieved contentment that a man might wear in the company of some forgotten boyhood friend whom he has just met by accident.

Beard was a happy man, too. Kenworthy had progressed with him. The quarryman was to a large extent the unfair victim of his craggy appearance; and even at this late leisure hour, presumably having come out two or three hours earlier to unwind, he was still clothed for his life-long fight with the rock-face: huge, scuffed, lime-dusty boots with great knots in their leather laces. We had noticed that Will Beard was not popular with his contemporaries. It was understandable. I did not think him a pugnacious man, in that he did not go about stirring up trouble. But he could be touchy, was slow to grasp new meanings, easily misunderstood what was said to him, mistook friendly wit for aggression and was apt to decide impulsively on reprisals. Moreover, he could have taken on any other two average Peak Lowites simultaneously.

But Kenworthy had already found the way into his confidence. Beard was evidently enjoying getting to know his first detective.

'It's funny, you know, Mr Kenworthy. I've read stories about Scotland Yard. And it's all looking at things through magnifying glasses and following people up back alleys. But with you – you know the ins and outs of a cat's arse-hole – you know everything that's been going on.'

Kenworthy drew me into the field.

'Here's another of us, Will. Shiner's just had a happy day in Lancashire, reconstructing a cat's arse-hole there. I've no doubt he's going to have a lot to tell us about the man with the car.'

164

Beard looked at me with a moonbeam smile of welcome into his circle.

'Tell Shiner about that car, Will.'

Beard first picked the gummed edge of his cigarette-paper. Not exactly a dull-witted man. I suppose, educationally, he might have been labelled sub-normal, but I would challenge the justice of that. The E.S.N. has block and limitations; but Will Beard could cover astonishing distances, given abundant time.

'It's a bloody silly car,' he said. 'What's anybody want to paint a car all them colours for?'

'Tell Shiner how many times you've seen that car in Peak Low.'

'Three,' he said proudly.

'And tell him about the second time.'

'Oh, that was late one night, early last week. I was going round for a Jimmy Riddle. And this chap asked me about the young lady who was up at the Bagshaws'.'

I had already told Kenworthy on the phone that Dugdale had been the driver on that occasion. Kenworthy leaned his head back on the wall behind him and partially closed his eyes.

'Now tell Shiner about the third time.'

'It was on the morning that the young lady got killed.'

'Will isn't exactly what you'd call a gossip,' Kenworthy said. 'He doesn't talk much to people. Therefore they don't mistake his motives. He thinks.'

'It was driving the back way up to Starvelings.'

'Which answers a question we've been asking ourselves ever since square one, Shiner. Who could have tempted Julie down Drydale at dawn? Someone she'd no reason to be afraid of. I think that would hold true, whether it was Dugdale or Caley who was at the wheel.'

He opened his brief-case and brought out three clips of paper, shuffled them so that a particular one was on top, and handed them to me.

'Have a quick glance.'

The top one was an abstract of a file that had been opened on Will Beard on a sexual assault complaint in the early months of 1939.

'Will was on leave from the Pioneer Corps – his first leave, he hadn't been in uniform long – the week that that other girl was killed,' Kenworthy said.

'Mason, her name was,' Beard interposed. 'Sally Mason.'

The girl whose father had laid an information to the police sergeant at Peak Forest had been a twelve-year-old called Mavis Weston. Mavis Weston had entered a field to look for cowslips, but finding none had wandered in her search further from the village than was permitted by repeated parental injunction. On a footpath skirting a wing of the Quarries she had met Beard, who had asked her what she was doing, and had offered to show her where she could find what she was looking for.

'Will,' Kenworthy said, cutting across my lines of thought, 'has his own theory about what happened to Sally Mason. Only he's not a man who goes about talking to all and sundry about his ideas.'

'It doesn't pay, Mr Kenworthy. People get hold of the wrong end of the stick.'

'Will can tell us that Julie was right about one thing. Sally Mason's officer *had* come back. Will had been in the army three months by now. He knew an officer when he saw one. He knows all about officers, does Will.'

'Shit-houses,' Beard said, factually and without rancour.

The previous year – it came as an absurd surprise

that the spring of 1939 had come only twelve months before the spring of 1940, the two worlds were so different – Will Beard had for some reason sat down with Mavis Weston, with their backs against a dry-stone wall.

I was struggling to follow two stories at once.

'Will was up and about early that morning, enjoying being home on leave, the ash-buds shooting, the curlew back after the winter. Also I fancy he was doing some illicit rabbiting, but that's something on which he prefers not to commit himself. He does however admit that he ran into Second Lieutenant J. T. R. Kirkland, who was looking for Drydale – and going in completely the wrong direction.'

'Didn't know whether his arse-hole was punched, bored, counter-sunk or reamered.'

I tried to keep one eye on Beard's face, and one on the typescript in front of me. He had not denied that his hands had strayed as he had sat with Mavis Weston in the lee of the wall. He had first put his palm over her knuckles, to show that he wanted to be friendly, and she had not objected to this. But when he had tried to put his arm about her shoulder, she had taken fright, had tried to jump to her feet, which was not an easy manoeuvre from the position in which she was sitting. Beard claimed that he at once released her, but admitted that in the untidy movement that followed – it hardly merited being called a scuffle – he had touched parts of her body that he should not have done.

'So Will sent Lieutenant Kirkland on his way,' Kenworthy said, 'though he isn't clear about what time it was – which is understandable. And he can't remember whether it was before or after he came across Jack Cantrell, sitting in a rock shelter on the east bank of

Drydale. But he did see a soldier, having a hand-to-hand affray with Julie Patterson in the bottom of the valley. He thought they were playing.'

As he had played with Mavis Weston? The sergeant who had dealt with the case had clearly been a shrewd and stolid observer. It was true that the back of Beard's hand brushed against the girl's growing breast as she was struggling up from beside him, but there was neither evidence nor suggestion that he had tried to interfere with her in any other way. The girl's frock was badly torn, but only at the back, and in a manner consonant with being dragged against the rough stones as she tried to stand up.

'So what Will has told us doesn't really settle anything. But I've told him how helpful it is. Isn't it, Shiner?'

'Immensely helpful,' I said.

The second clip of papers consisted of Telex messages from the Artillery Records Office at Foots Cray.

> *5960556 KIRKLAND, John Trevor Ryder, 2 Lt R.A. Missing; believed killed in action, Albert Canal, Belgium, 12th May, 1940.*

That was barely a week after his first appearance in Peak Low, but an attached note provided an explanation. For some two months he had held supernumerary rank with a training regiment on Salisbury Plain, to which he had been posted on leaving O.C.T.U. It must have been from there that he had travelled up to the High Peak on short pass. But no sooner was he back at Larkhill than he received an emergency posting as a replacement with the Expeditionary Force. His official destination was a division that was on the move on the day of his arrival. Military conditions were charitably described as 'fluid'; the transit column with which he was endeavouring to reach the operational zone ran into several bursts of trouble as the main German push south-westwards gathered momentum. It was ultimately destroyed by dive-bombers, its personnel either killed on the spot or scattered.

'So what do you make of that?'

Kenworthy had noted that I was reading the document a second time, and he did not seem at all worried at talking about it in front of Beard.

'I suppose he could have seen his chance and come back – in the confusion.'

'Impulse, probably. What mental agony, knowing that Sally was stuck here.'

'But could he have crossed the Channel?'

'He could if he'd used his loaf. There were ways and means.'

I remembered that Kenworthy had been in France in those days.

'But if he'd left it any longer, it would have been touch and go whether he would ever have reached the coast. We shall never know, Shiner.'

Will Beard was looking at us with smiling interest. We were talking fast, and I did not know whether he was really following us or not.

'Shiner, I think this settles another thing that's been puzzling me. I can see him, at his wit's end, and perhaps half out of his mind at his first whiff of action, chucking a dummy – deserting, let's call it what it was – to come back here to marry Sally. But not to kill her.'

'How much evidence have we got that he did kill her? Only our own reading of Julie's original supposition. And that's only based on the way we think she edited a folk-legend – '

I really did think that Kenworthy was now going too far with this. It was all hypothetical: feasible, tempting, even enjoyable, taken as mental exercise. But wasn't Kenworthy whole-hogging it too much, behaving as if he were convinced of it to the exclusion of all other possibilities? He was now leaning forward, positively scowling at me, nearly at the end of his patience, dangerously near to anger at my scepticism. I saw for the first time his nerves breaking through: a gambler's nerves.

'Don't you *see*, Shiner? Maybe we are still testing a theory. But don't you see that that theory has just had the mightiest fillip? When you phoned me from Halliton, earlier this evening, and told me what Dugdale had said, you told me that Julie had told him that she had changed her mind. What were her actual words?'

I found them in my notes.

'It was a funny thing, but she now knew she had been wrong all these years – about who had killed Sally Mason. And Dugdale answered, "Julie, I didn't come here to talk about that." '

'Exactly. Don't you see that that reinforces our original impression?'

'It might,' I said.

'Keep it up, Shiner. Bloody good show! That's what sergeants are for – to stop inspectors from making damned fools of themselves. If you're doing your job properly, your life and mine together will be one long bloody row. But you can give this one a rest, here and now, because, say what you like, I'm putting my shirt on it. Julie Wimpole went through most of her adult life believing that Kirkland killed Sally Mason. She picked up something the week before last that convinced her he hadn't.'

'So what happened to Kirkland? I know some deserters managed to go to ground for the duration and beyond. But Kirkland was surely out of that class.'

'The same thing happened to Kirkland as happened to Walter Chapman.'

'Walter Chapman? Are we back with Mary Booth-royd now, then? Can't we leave the eighteenth century out of it? We're in a bad enough tangle as it is.'

And Kenworthy suddenly changed his mood again.

'Shiner, I'm not going to say yet whether I hope you'll ever work with me again. But if you ever do, I'll promise you one thing. It won't always be like this.'

Then he turned back to Will Beard. I don't know what Beard could possibly have made of that inter-change. Perhaps it was as well that he was not a gossip.

'Ah well, Will Beard's been very helpful up to now,' Kenworthy said. 'Maybe he can go on being helpful.'

And Beard looked back at us hopefully. His face was scarred by rock-chips and beaten by decades of fell weathers, but he was aiming at an expression of seraphic simplicity.

'Let's go back to the first night Julie arrived in Peak Low, shall we?'

'She sat next to me on the bus.'

'You mean, you sat next to her. Did you know who it was you were sitting next to?'

'The bus was pretty full, Mr Kenworthy. I took the first empty seat.'

'But you knew as soon as she started talking to you, didn't you, where you'd heard her voice before? At least, you must have wondered.'

'I did wonder, Mr Kenworthy.'

Kenworthy grinned at him.

'Funny how things sometimes escape you, isn't it? Like trying to put a name to a face, or a tune. Only I don't think somehow that Julie would have much difficulty in placing you.'

171

Beard faced that one out in a silence that might have gone on for a long time.

'So just run over again for us all the things you talked about that night on your way up to Starvelings. Or wait: answer me another question first. Why do you think Cantrell tried so hard to go up to the farm with her instead of you?'

'I don't know, Mr Kenworthy. Without he thought – '

'Without he thought what?'

'Without he thought I was a bit of a rough diamond for the lady.'

'Or do you think it was because he didn't want her to have the chance to talk to you?'

There was a familiar insistence creeping into his tone, but he had not yet reached his show-down style. Beard could again find nothing to say to the question.

'Why do you think Jack Cantrell didn't want Julie to have the chance to talk to you?'

'Can't think, Mr Kenworthy.'

'So let's just run over it again, shall we, all that you talked about?'

We had it all again: how she had asked about the Keelings of Bracken Farm, who had moved away before the end of the war; and about the Powder Mill, and how it had once been a school, and how you could burn a five-barred gate in some of its fireplaces.

'And the rest,' Kenworthy snapped.

'I don't know what you mean, the rest.'

'I can hardly believe that Julie Wimpole missed the opportunity to talk about Drydale.'

'We just happened to say how dry it still was for the time of the year.'

'Unusual, is it?'

'We'd had a pretty dry autumn, until a few days ago.'

'And 1940 was a pretty dry spring, too, wasn't it?'

Kenworthy said that more as if he were talking to himself. And at this moment we had an interruption. Hepplewhite had opened the door of his private quarters and come into the space behind the bar.

'If any of you gentlemen fancy a drink – '

'No. Just leave us alone.'

Kenworthy surprised me by being so peremptory. Hepplewhite slunk away cowed. Kenworthy brought out Julie's notebook, smoothed down a page, and set it down in front of Beard. I noticed that he kept his fingers firmly on it.

'Julie drew that one day the week before last.'

The shepherd's hut and the tumble of stones at its lower end. For the first time, I saw fear in Beard's eyes. There was a marked change in him. I could see him weighing up the disposition of the furniture between him and the door. I weighed it up, too. I wasn't at all keen on mixing it with Will Beard.

'Julie talked to you about that, too, the night you carried her suitcase, didn't she? When she was asking you where the river goes to in a dry spring?'

Beard moistened his lips.

'I didn't have anything to do with that, Mr Kenworthy.'

'Thank you very much, Will,' Kenworthy said, but did not tell him what for. 'So in that case you won't mind helping us to move the stone, will you?'

Beard suddenly appeared to have been deprived of both speech and emotion. Kenworthy slid the sketch an inch or two nearer to him.

'Which stone was it, Will?'

'I don't know what you're talking about.'

'You did a couple of minutes ago.'

But that was too near to reasoning to succeed with

Will Beard. Kenworthy let silence develop – a long, idle silence, in which we became aware for the first time of the sounds of the inn: a jet of flame burning from a lump of bituminous coal on the fire; a cheap tin clock, ticking somewhere behind the bar, the drip of a beer-tap into an ullage can. Kenworthy got up and walked about the room. I turned to the third of the documents that he had handed to me.

> *There are a thousand paths to the delectable tavern of death, and some run straight and some run crooked.*
> *The quotation is taken from James Elroy Flecker's* Hassan, *Act II Scene ii. The words are spoken by the Caliph and have no more profundity than their surface meaning: a suggestion of the inexorability of fate.*

We heard Hepplewhite moving about again. But this time he opened and shut several doors, approaching us through the public entrance, on which he had the prudence to knock.

'I don't want to make a nuisance of myself, gentlemen, but I'm wanting my bed.'

'Go to bed, then. Lock us in, if you like. We're going to be here all night.'

'I don't know what I've done to deserve this.'

When he had gone, Kenworthy began pointedly ignoring Beard. He started talking to me again, intimate considerations about the case, which he did not in the least seem to mind Beard hearing.

'There was something we overlooked in that notebook of Julie's, Shiner. We ought to have paid more attention to the order in which those items of poetry came. There's progression there. I can see it now. I thought at first she was, like the scholar says, just contemplating the inexorability of fate. But I'm beginning to think differently. *Nurse, oh my love is slain*: wondering

174

whether Harbutt's going to turn up to marry her or not. Then *Hamlet*: the agony of slow decision: whether to be there herself if he did. Then the three names:

M. Boothroyd

S. Mason

J. Wimpole?

I thought at first she was half crazed, contemplating her own demise. The same with *the delectable tavern of death*. But I don't think she was. I think she was congratulating herself on her narrow escape. Half a pint of milk on the Friday morning and away.'

Speculation: I was beginning to be physically nauseated by it. How the hell could we ever know? And where could it possibly lead us?

'Another thing we've overlooked, Shiner, is that boys and grown men can be as fond of crude herd-sport as any pack of school girls. Early one May morning, just as the sun was rising – I don't think Will Beard was the only one out poaching – were you, Will?'

Beard looked at him with eyes that rolled sickly and savagely in their sockets.

'I said, were you, Will? Who was out rabbiting with you, that day you ran into the officer?'

'Not rabbiting. Rook-shooting.'

'Rook-shooting, then.'

'There was Bill Hepplewhite, Arthur Rousell, one or two others.'

'And the officer asked you the way?'

'I've already told you. He didn't know whether his – '

'A memorable phrase. I've no doubt you've used it every time you've ever spoken of him. Spare us the repetition. It won't advance us. What I'm getting at is, you were no better than the girls. You saw the chance of a bit of a leg-pull, too. Especially a rather lah-di-dah

one-pipper, whom you've already elegantly charac-
terised. You can spare us a repetition of that one, too.
You sent him down Drydale. He didn't ask you the
way. He didn't know about Drydale, until you told him
that that was where the girls had sent Sally. Then you
stalked him down there yourselves, to have your bit of
fun – play-acting: dishing up Walter Chapman and
Mary Boothroyd over again. Only it went a bit too far,
didn't it, Will? Accidentally?'

I have often wondered how long a really determined
suspect could hold out in silence. I had begun to think
that Will Beard was going to defeat us. It was that
Accidentally that had lured him on to the reef. That and
Kenworthy's offer of something he could honestly
refute.

'Lieutenant Kirkland and Sally Mason might have
been an accident, but Julie Wimpole wasn't.'

'I didn't kill her.'

'I *know* you didn't, Will. Can't you see that's the one
thing I've believed all along?'

Beard looked as if he found this confidence even
more tempting, but he still clung to some distrust. I
can't say I blamed him.

'Who is not for us is against us,' Kenworthy said, but
I do not think that Beard took this in.

'What I mean is, unless you tell us which stone, I shall
begin to think that you really have something to hide.'

Beard blinked. Then slowly his finger moved.

'This one here. But it will be full of water by now.'

'In which case, we shall need frogmen as well as the
Cave Rescue team.'

Then he turned to me.

'You didn't do badly in that last interview with
Dugdale, Shiner – but you missed out two key questions. When he came back from that Tuesday night

visit, did he go and see Harbutt again? I think he would, don't you? I think he'd make one more effort to talk decency into Harbutt. I think it would be a fairly placid interview, because Dugdale had a professional relationship with Harbutt – and Dugdale strikes me as a man who would always be ultra-careful about professional relationships. So maybe they talked in a general way about Julie – and the role of Peak Low in her life. So might Dugdale possibly have mentioned in passing that Julie now said she had changed her mind about who had killed Sally? I can think of a dozen ways in which the subject might have come up. And if it did, Harbutt would surely have found it highly disturbing.'

CHAPTER EIGHTEEN

I had thought that Kenworthy's remark to the landlord about our spending the night in his bar had just been part of the current no-change-for-Hepplewhite campaign. But it soon became clear that this was precisely what we were going to do. There was a public coin-box telephone in the pub entrance and Kenworthy spent some time at this, leaving me to keep silent watch over Beard.

It was mostly a silent watch, and the most striking feature was Beard's apparently meek acceptance of the situation. He did not ask if he could go home. He did not show any aggression. At one point he looked at me with the expression of a dog that knows it gets kicked on occasion, but is also confident of subsistence rations at irregular but salutary intervals.

'What's going to happen now?' he asked me.

'That's up to Kenworthy.'

'I didn't kill the one they called Julie.'

'Kenworthy seems to believe that.'

After some twenty minutes, Kenworthy returned, nodded to me that he was satisfied with what he had just transacted, and told me to try to get some sleep. He would wake me for a spell if he felt he needed a doze himself. In fact, he didn't. I cat-napped off and on, and whenever I looked up across the dingy room, he appeared to be writing. Will Beard spread his arms on the table and flattened his cheek on them. Whether he was actually asleep or not, I could not say, but he did not seem to move for at least four hours.

At half past six Hepplewhite visited us in bedroom slippers and dressing-gown, his hair thin but unkempt, the beginnings of a corporation sagging over his pyjama girdle. He opened the street door long enough to let a cat in, switched on lights in the kitchen behind the bar, filled a kettle, and then came out again with empty milk-bottles.

'I can do you a breakfast if you like.'

'We'd be grateful,' Kenworthy said. 'And I should fuel up myself, if I were you. You're coming for a walk with us.'

He nudged Will Beard, who came to life with some confusion at first, but eventually seemed to comprehend where he was and why, and had no comment to make on it.

We could smell the bacon and eggs before Hepplewhite appeared with them. He brought them with thick wedges of bread and butter and strong tea.

'I don't know what he's been telling you,' Hepplewhite attempted.

'I'm sure you'd like to qualify it with your own version.'

'I'm saying nothing.'

'Yet.'

The three of us ate together. Transport pulled up in front of the inn. Kenworthy got up to go to the door. But first there were two points that he still needed to tidy up with Beard. It was the only time throughout the meal that he referred to the case.

'There's one thing that you haven't really made clear to us, Will. We know that you and Julie had a good old talk on the way to Starvelings that first night. But did you see anything else of Julie during her stay here?'

'She was lying in wait for me one afternoon when I got off the bus.'

'And she got you to tell her which stone it was, and all that?'

'She worried it out of me.'

'I'll bet she did. And she was going to get you to move it for her?'

'I kept out of her way, after that. In any case, after all this rain – it's a waste of time, you know.'

'We'll see.'

Kenworthy opened the street door to the new arrivals. It was a spear-head working team of a local Cave Rescue society; men in miners' helmets with lamps over their foreheads, ropes about their shoulders and various implements in their belts. Their leader was brisk; and clearly out, amongst other things, to enjoy himself.

'Waterswallow down in Drydale, I believe?'

'Below the old shepherd's hut. You know it?'

'I've seen it. None of us have ever been in there. And after the storms we've been having – '

'We shall have to take a chance on that.'

'We've brought hand-pumps. We might be able to get the level down a foot or two.'

'We'll see,' Kenworthy said. It appeared to have become his motto this morning.

Within minutes a miscellaneous police contingent arrived. Kenworthy extracted a slip of paper from his notebook and handed it to the uniformed inspector.

'These are the chaps I want rounded up. No questions answered, except that they're coming with us. No private consultation between them, please, but comments in public needn't be discouraged, could be informative, everything to be noted down. Put somebody reliable on to that.'

Kenworthy stroked his bristly chin.

'Better go and get a shave, Shiner. You'll feel fresher for it. Myself, I'm going to play the worn-out hatchet-face who's been up all night. As indeed I am and have been. You can give yourself ten minutes.'

Fatigue and excited alertness alternated in me in waves. Both Kenworthy and I were accustomed to being in the red on our sleep now and then; we were still both young and fit enough to afford the interest on the overdraft.

If Peak Low was watching us assemble and move off from our start-line, then the village was being even more than usually circumspect about its curiosity. Perhaps they did not want to know. Many of the bedroom curtains, and most of those in the downstairs windows, were still drawn and there was not an inhabitant in sight, except those that Kenworthy had drawn out: Hepplewhite and Beard, Rousell and a couple of the rock-face workmen who had always been evident, though unnamed and relatively featureless in the group to whom we had frequently listened in the public bar.

The early bus had arrived in the village and was reversing at the cross-roads, its lighted interior looking indefinably incongruous against the background of grey stone cottages. Passengers had not yet begun to arrive for it, and its driver and conductor were following our movements with open interest.

In a long, loose column we straggled along a lane through a stile into a wet and uninviting field. It was no longer actually raining, but the earth was spongy and the slope towards the head of the dale was intersected with a network of unmapped rivulets.

Kenworthy had sent the rescue team on ahead, because they had heavy equipment to carry. They were under instructions to touch nothing and start nothing until we arrived. The policemen and our group of villagers were loosely intermingled. No one was under arrest; anyone reluctant to accompany us would have lost his objection – but only after the sort of altercation which Kenworthy was anxious not to have at this juncture. As it was he was playing in reverse on the very same herd instinct that had got these men into this situation in the first instance. Not one of them now dared break away, for fear of what the others might say in his absence. To have done so would have been a tacit admission of guilt. And I know now, looking back, that there was one hope, unexpressed but latent in every one of them: that once the stone was moved the whole expedition would prove futile. A great deal of that leaden hope was attached to the flood-level of the underground watercourse. I think we all of us – cave-hunters, suspects, Kenworthy and I – had our fingers crossed about that – for three different sets of motives.

We looked down at the torrent under the plank bridge. I tried to decide – though it was impossible to arrive at any sort of scientific certainty – whether the level of the water had changed since I had last been here. That swirling current round the tip of a boulder that a week ago had been exposed – was there more or less of it visible now than there had been the other morning, when Kenworthy and I had had our cold, wet walk? I tried to convince myself that there was no great difference.

We tramped across the planks: Kenworthy, Hepple-white, quarrymen, Beard, and police. Down into the valley we each tended to choose a different track to avoid boggy patches and slithering stretches of exposed rock. The Peak Low men were not talking to each other at all, but they were walking now together in a bunch, with the exception of Will Beard, who was attached to none of them. I noticed that a uniformed police sergeant had clearly marked him, and was keeping unobtrusively but doggedly on his heels.

When we approached the ruin, Kenworthy, who had been leading us with long, lolloping strides, almost running in his impatience, turned and waited for me, picking up one of the fallen stones, examining it and then casting it away – a repetition of the mime he had gone through before, imitating the way in which Julie was said to have behaved. For the first time, he addressed himself to one of the village men.

'You, Rousell – it was you who told us about that – about watching Julie, that first morning. I'm surprised that you did.'

He now spoke to the whole group.

'In fact, I'm surprised at you all. Over-confidence, that's what it was. It wasn't a bad act, all told, the way you knew nothing, except what you could have been expected to have seen. You didn't even recognise the woman with the stammer. Because, of course, there were plenty of newcomers in Peak Low, like the secretary of the Women's Institute, who didn't know her. All you had to do was to think yourselves into a position of general ignorance, and play it from there.

But you, Rousell – to tell us how she actually handled one of the stones – I suppose you thought it was a master-stroke of innocent realism. It never pays to be clever, Rousell, old son. That's how they all come unstuck.'

'I had nothing to do with that business,' Rousell said. 'I just happened to be there, that was all.'

'Yes. That's what you're all going to say. There was a Rousell who just happened to be there in the eighteenth century, too. And a Hepplewhite. Shall I tell you what the judge is going to say on that point in his summing-up? Or will you wait to hear it for yourselves?'

He turned to me. 'Now I know why Julie picked that stone up and played with it. She was getting the feel of it – the weight – deciding that it was beyond her strength to shift the one that mattered.'

And he went and slapped with the flat of his hand a boulder that protruded from a spit of ground skirted by the river on the southern end of the ruin. It was one that had been heavily shaded in the sketch in Julie's notebook.

'Come along, Will. Let's see what you're made of.'

Beard stood motionless, undetermined whether to mutiny or not. The others stood silently watching him. One could read their minds: Beard was a bloody fool, always had been. If Beard had only kept his bloody mouth shut! Yet there was still a hope: that Beard would refuse to co-operate (which need only delay us for minutes), that even when the stone was shifted, there would be nothing but water, till May or June of next year, at least. They must have known, theoretically, of frog men, but we hadn't one with us, and irrational mob optimism died hard.

'Come on, Will.'

Beard's hands rose and fell at his sides.

'Will – I do believe you don't think you can do it.'

A vague stir amongst the others, a consciousness of Kenworthy's unsportsmanlike methods.

'Who isn't for us is against us, Will.'

The others stood stock-still. Beard advanced towards the stone, ignoring the rest of them, clasped his arms round it from two or three tentative angles. I looked at the semi-circle of faces, the policemen now forming an outer ring behind them. They were taking care now not to look at each other.

Was this how it had been on that May morning, seventeen years ago? Was it Beard they had relied on then, to shift the boulder for them, exposing the sub-terranean swallet that they all knew about, as vaguely and yet as surely as they knew Tuppy Ibberson's story about Walter Chapman and Mary Boothroyd?

Beard found the angle that suited him, adjusted his footing, embraced the stone with a false show of loving, as might a woolly and angry bear with his victim. And then there was a rending sound like the roots of a molar coming out of their bed-socket at the twist of a dentist's forceps. The stone moved an inch. A policeman stepped forward and tore away an exposed hawthorn root that was trapping one of its corners. Beard tipped the boulder back on the fulcrum of its lower corner, and stood away from a gaping hole panting, his face flushed and savage. There was the sound of a rushing cascade at our feet.

Kenworthy signalled to the leader of the rescue team, who went forward on his hands and knees with one of his mates. For silent seconds they crouched, peering inwards and down; and then the first man began to crawl forward, his torso disappearing down-wards at an angle of forty-five degrees.

There he seemed at first to become stuck. Then he wriggled partially out and called for more light. An encased car head lamp was passed to him, and connected to a heavy-duty accumulator. He crept forward again, stuck at first for some moments in the position he had first reached. Then his legs began to wriggle, and first his knees, then his ankles, then the soles of his boots disappeared from our sight. His companion eased himself down behind him. Not one of the others took a step closer.

I looked at Kenworthy. He was standing with shadows of beard round his jaws, his eyes bloodshot as if in dynamic victory over the weariness of the flesh.

Presently the second man came out, feet first, nodded to us as if to assure us of success, but giving no details. His leader followed almost immediately.

'It's very wet down there. What we call a wet curtain. You can hear it. But it isn't flooded. It never could be. It's too deep. There's too much clearance. It must be the key to a whole system. And there's something you ought to see – '

This was to Kenworthy.

'You'll get soaked. But I think it's what you came for.'

Kenworthy went on all fours, groaned as the rubble rolled painfully under his body, and began to edge himself into the hole.

'I've fixed the lamp on a ledge for you. Be careful not to knock it. It's beamed on an exhibit.'

Kenworthy seemed gone for a very long time. When he returned, he had managed to turn over on to his back, so that his lean and angry face was looking up at the sky as he emerged. I helped him to his feet.

'Right. You're all going to look at that. One at a time. Hepplewhite, you first.'

Then it was, 'William John Hepplewhite, I am arresting you for the murder in May 1940 of Sarah Antonia Mason and John Trevor Ryder Kirkland. You are not obliged to say anything. Arthur Rousell – '

One at a time, four of them re-emerged, ashen, trembling, drenched, cold and silent. The world had changed so much since this had all happened. As Kenworthy had once said, they had all been places since then: the African desert, the Western Approaches, the *bocage* of Normandy. It was as if nothing of May 1940 had even the right to remain.

'All right, Sergeant Wright, it's absolutely unnecessary for you to go too. But if I don't let you see it with your own eyes, you'll never forgive me.'

Loose peebles grated under my kneecaps. The full force of the waterfall soaked my left side. But to my right there was a space. I eased myself over. Water was dripping all round me from a curtain of stalactites.

And what was I expecting to see? Some dramatic relic of evidence, perhaps? Bones? A skull? Hardly a recognisable skeleton, unless remnants of clothing had held the frame together. And what state would khaki serge be in, after all those years in all that moisture? The last thing for which I was prepared was an identifiable human body. But that was what the beam of light was playing on, lying on a ledge in a pool of water of whose depth I could not be certain – like the tomb of a crusader whose features have been chipped away and worn smooth. An arm, which had fallen to hang over the edge of the niche, was hanging with the cuff of the tunic and grotesquely deformed fingers starkly delineated. The peak and crown of a military uniform cap appeared to be growing out of the stone.

Second Lieutenant Kirkland was encased in a deposit of stalagmatic carbonates. In the nineteenth century, we later learned, amongst the wonders of the High Peak at the height of its hydropathic popularity, had been its petrifying wells. There was a record of a visit to one of them at Matlock by the Princess Victoria in 1832. There is so much mineral salt in suspension in the water that it quickly forms a crust round objects immersed in it. Birds' nests, cutlery and ornamental baskets were left by tourists to be turned into stone. And this is what had happened to Sally Mason's lieutenant. God knows what state the body would be in when its coating was chipped away.

'Well,' Kenworthy said. 'I've already told you. Nobody is obliged to say anything. And in fact, if I were you – '

'It was all a big bloody accident,' Hepplewhite said. 'We never meant any harm. *He's* the only one who did murder – '

I thought we might have to restrain him from an attack on Will Beard.

'We were out rook-shooting. Will Beard was home on leave. All lads together. Then we saw this second lieutenant, lah-di-dah type, bloody pansy, we thought. He'd hitched a lift on some army transport that dropped him off in the village. Was setting out, obviously, for Ada Bramwell's, where he was expecting to find the girl. Well, we knew, you see, though we weren't supposed to, but things get about in a village, about the trick the girls were going to play on her. We'd seen her set out for the valley, so we told him that was where she had gone. He set out like a bloody hare, and we decided to cut him off and have our own bit of fun. We know a thing or two about footpaths and short cuts, you understand. But we didn't mean any harm. I mean, a couple getting wed, they're good for a laugh at the best of times, aren't they?'

Kenworthy was silent. Laughter had been an unfortunate thing to mention.

'Well, we got down here pretty well as soon as he did, since we knew how to cut out the bend in the dale. The girl was sitting by the ruin waiting for him, because for some reason or other the school girls' caper hadn't come off. She sprang up when she saw him, and started to run towards him, and we all came careering down the slope, yelling like Red Indians, pretending we were like that lot in the old legend – Tuppy Ibberson's tale.'

Not one of the others made any sign of wanting to deny it.

'But we'd reckoned without that second lieutenant. We didn't think he was going to fight back, not against five of us. But he did; and he went for Will, because Will happened to be in the lead. And if we thought he was a pansy, we were bloody mistaken. He knew ju-jitsu, or something. He had Will down in a sort of Judo throw, and then he lunged at me with his shoulder. But then, of course, Will got his gander up, lowered the boom, got hold of that officer with a strength that no man could oppose. He broke his bloody neck just by shaking him. We heard the spine-bones crack. And the girl screamed – Will picked up a stone and did for her, just as she was found. Just like Tuppy had always told us about that other girl.'

The Cave Rescue leader was looking lovingly at the exposed hole. For him this was the chance of a lifetime. Kenworthy nodded permission.

Hepplewhite continued. 'Then suddenly, we see this soldier. He's the one who's been flogging the knives. And he's sleeping out with Aggie Heathcote, whose old man's away in the Merchant Navy. We knew about that, of course; but also, he'd just seen all that had happened. And never in my life have I seen a man so

cool. He came down to us slowly, swaggering, actually
smiling. And he went straight up to that officer's body,
opened the tunic pockets, and helped himself to what
was in his wallet. And that was a fair old whack,
because he was going to get married, and there was
enough ready cash for a week on the spree.'

' "You didn't see this," he said. "And I didn't see
that." '

'Then we bethought ourselves that there was supposed to be a swallet just under and past the ruin. It
was said to be bigger and deeper than most in the dale.
And Will Beard, he seemed to know where it was, anyway, and he started to shift the stone, just as he did just
now. Then the soldier cottoned on to what was happening, and he said, "Look, I've got to be back in my own
bed for roll-call at reveille, but I'll stand guard up
yonder for ten minutes, in case anyone comes down. So
get cracking." Some of us wanted to put the girl's body
down the hole too – if we had, the chances are that none
of this would ever have come to light. But some stupid
sod – it was you, Arthur – said, "No, let's leave it like
history over again." '

Kenworthy looked at Arthur Rousell.

'I'll be buggered if it was my idea,' Rousell said. 'We
were all in it together. And we were past thinking of
anything new. But I'll tell you one thing, Mr Kenworthy, it's not us you want for Julie Wimpole. It's that
bloody soldier. *He* was there that morning. You can't
do much in this village without it being known, and he
came in that Friday, driving that crazy bloody car. It
was parked in a spinney behind Starvelings, the time
she was being done in.'

This left us with a puzzle. We thought that by the
time of the arrival of that car in Peak Low, Julie had
decided that Harbutt was involved to some atrocious

extent in the killing of Sally Mason. Julie had heard Sally scream – but it had not been, as Harbutt had told us, while she was talking to him on his feigned sentry-duty. We now knew that this could not be so. So it must have been earlier. And she must have accepted his tale that he had been posted where he was by the officer. So she also accepted that the officer must be the murderer: and, by parallel, thought that that was what had probably happened in the eighteenth-century story, too. Not a logical inference; but Julie Wimpole's logic was not impeccable.

But how had Harbutt, that Friday morning, managed to lure her into Drydale? She could only have gone with him voluntarily. The fact remained that she had. She had already been passionately, as we thought, insanely in love with him. How that love had been crushed by his incrimination in the Sally Mason murder was something that we could only imagine. Harbutt had the gift of the gab; he had clearly come back to Peak Low, that May morning, with a line ready to shoot. 'Come down to Drydale with me, then, and I'll show you something that proves my innocence.' Something like that? What else could it be? Had her infatuation not been finally crushed? Had Harbutt the secret of still making her pause? Was her sense of fairness and poetry such that she gave him yet another chance? In the face of her common sense? Julie's common sense had failed her more than once, to our knowledge. There was a lot about her psychology that we could never claim even to begin to be sure about.

We were never to know. The only man who might have told us was Harbutt himself; and his defence throughout was denial and silence. He did not admit anything – not even the theft of the money from Kirkland, in the evidence of five eye-witnesses. He pleaded not guilty and his counsel, obviously, kept him out of the witness-box. There was no condemned cell confession. The jury deliberated for five hours and twenty-six minutes; one supposes that they were swayed by the consideration that he had made the night journey over the moors in an invidiously recognisable car that he had 'borrowed' from a town waste-heap. The ignition key would have given no difficulty to a man of his specialisms.

Kenworthy spoke to the uniformed inspector, who now detailed his cohort with military precision. Our file back up Drydale was a good deal more formal than our descent had been.

The head and shoulders of the cave-rescuer appeared from the chasm.

'Something else down here, Mr Kenworthy.'

I saw nothing to startle me at first: Walter Chapman had been down there a good deal longer than Lieutenant Kirkland. There were blobs and excrescences of deposit, discoloured by streaks of mineral solutions, some of them fortuitously similar to commonplace objects. In the show caves the guides have the silly habit of giving them names for the amusement of tourists: like poached eggs, beehives and candlesticks. There was one such formation like the scalloped edge of an exotic sea-shell. But it needed an imagination as fertile as Kenworthy's to pronounce it a frilly laced cuff. The knuckles of the hand beneath it were completely obliterated under the ubiquitous eroding stone; but they were there, right enough, when we returned at leisure to chisel them out. And there was no mistaking the form of the tricorn hat which I suddenly saw, where it had fallen a few yards away from its owner's corpse, its dented crown and jaunty rim faithfully preserved under the guardianship of the lime.

'I said we might be lucky with this case, Shiner.'

'Yes, sir.'

'Nine blind bastards, Shiner.'

'Sir.'